FALLEN ANGEL

DETECTIVE PAUL CULLEN MYSTERIES BOOK 2

PAUL PILKINGTON

First published 2020

This edition published 2023

Published by Fast Paced Fiction

Paperback ISBN: 978-1-915367-28-0

This novel is written in British (UK) English. British English words, spelling (favourite, colour, etc.) and grammar are used throughout.

Cover design by Jeanine Henning.

For my family and loyal readers

ALSO BY PAUL PILKINGTON

Detective Paul Cullen Mysteries:

Long Gone

Fallen Angel

Dead Ahead

Deep Sleeper

May Day (coming 2024)

Emma Holden Trilogy:

The One You Love

The One You Fear

The One You Trust

Standalone Novels:

Someone to Save You

I Heard You

For Your Own Protection

PART I

1

He followed the pretty oriental-looking girl with the pink suitcase all the way from Paddington to Piccadilly Circus. He hadn't intended to follow a girl today, but just the sight of her, her beauty, her exotic-ness, was irresistible. She wore a comfy black tracksuit, with gold trim, which hugged the curves of her body. Her dark silken hair was tied back into a playful ponytail that swung left and right as she walked, like a metronome.

She'd been making her way across the busy concourse at Paddington, first thing on Monday morning, looking every bit the new visitor, as the well-versed commuters hurried past, heads down in their phone screens.

She'd probably just arrived at Heathrow, after a long flight from Singapore, or China, or Malaysia. Maybe even Australia - they had a lot of oriental people there, he knew that. And yet she looked *so* good, despite what must have been a tiring journey. Long haul flights weren't good for your health, so he'd read. They dried out the skin.

But she looked so fresh. And lovely. Good enough to eat.

She'd consulted her phone, before heading down the short staircase to the Underground, before passing through the barriers towards the Bakerloo Line. He followed closely, comforted that she would never suspect a thing, such was the number of people down here. The tube was the perfect place for him, with hundreds, thousands of human shields allowing him to service his desires undisturbed.

He watched as she stepped onto the longer escalator which took passengers down to the lower levels of the Bakerloo Line. With her suitcase, she took up the whole of the escalator, and a queue of mildly annoyed people quickly built up behind her on the left.

It must be her first time in London, he thought. She didn't know about the protocol to stand on the right and leave the left-hand side clear for those in a hurry.

He watched as she realised, and shifted her case to the step directly in front of her.

You could tell a lot from people's small actions; how they behaved, their mannerisms, the micro-expressions. It could reveal a whole hidden world, and he felt privileged to spend time getting to know these people; every single one of them.

How he would love to get to know her better.

AS THEY REACHED the bottom of the escalator, he guessed which way she would be heading, and was correct when she headed right, southbound. He was only three people away from the girl, and as they emerged onto the platform they stood just a few metres apart. He ventured a sideways glance at her, taking in her beauty, as she tilted her beautiful head to read the train information board above them.

'Your next train to Elephant and Castle is due to arrive in two minutes,' the customer services host announced from just along the platform.

Two minutes. One hundred and twenty seconds. He could have gazed at this beautiful girl for the whole time, but he didn't want to put himself at risk. There was a CCTV camera just off towards the left, and he was right in its sights. In the control room at Paddington, someone was watching, flanked by a bank of screens, monitoring the masses for any suspicious activity.

He'd been more careful since the police operation had begun.

The posters were impossible to miss, showing a shadowy figure among the crowds, warning off possible offenders with the threat of arrest and prosecution.

And the police were serious. He'd read in the paper about the arrests that they had made as part of Operation Archangel. Men who had touched women, taking advantage of their vulnerability in the crowded, confined space of the tube train carriage. Pressing their hands against the warm bodies, pretending the contact was accidental.

That wasn't him. He wouldn't do that. But there was always the chance that he might be innocently caught up in the police net.

'Your train is about to arrive. Please stand behind the yellow line, for your own safety, and let the passengers off the train before boarding.'

He watched down the tunnel as the train appeared, its lights shining brightly in the gloom of London's manmade subterranean world.

'Please stand behind the yellow line,' the customer

service host repeated, as the passengers on the platform edged closer in anticipation of the train's arrival.

He imagined, as he often did, launching himself onto the tracks just as the train was speeding into the station, almost feeling the imaginary high velocity impact of metal on skin and bone.

How would it feel? Would there be pain? Or just darkness?

One day he might find out.

HE STEPPED onto the train right behind her, enjoying being so close yet so invisible. The carriage wasn't too busy, so the girl managed to get a seat, keeping the suitcase close. He took a seat opposite, but not directly in her line of vision. He would be able to watch better at more of an angle, where the chance of her spotting his interest would be less.

His eyes did a quick sweep of the half-full carriage. None of these people - the big black guy, eyes closed wearing oversized headphones, the young mother with pushchair and smiling baby girl, the older gentlemen reading a book - looked like transport police, but that was the point of plain clothes officers, wasn't it? He had to always assume that *someone* could be present, looking out.

He didn't want to be caught up in something he didn't deserve.

He stole several glances at the flawless girl, craving her, from across the carriage as the train rattled and squealed through the darkness of London's underground.

She was scrolling on her phone - the distance was too great for him to see exactly what she was doing - but he wondered whether she was messaging a friend, maybe a boyfriend.

He wondered about her life.

Where had she come from?

Where was she going?

He was so engrossed in these questions that he nearly missed her standing as the train rushed into Piccadilly Circus station. He followed her off the train, through the bustling station, up the escalator and into the brightness of the day in the heart of London's West End.

He stood at the side of the station entrance, the warmth of the early-morning sun on his face, as tourists meandered past him. There were plenty of pretty, young girls among the hordes, but he only had eyes for one.

The girl had paused about twenty metres away, consulting her phone again.

Maybe she was lost.

Maybe she was looking for a hotel.

He imagined her entering the hotel room, slipping off her jacket before throwing her body down on the bed, satin hair spreading out over the freshly laundered bed sheets, legs parted ever so slightly.

Waiting for him.

And then the girl burst to life as another girl, just as beautiful as his target, approached, arms outstretched, joy across her face. They embraced.

A friend.

The two girls kissed tenderly.

More than a friend...

He felt the anger smoulder deep inside him as he watched the two girls walk off, arms linked, shoulders touching. He traced their journey across the street, re-imagining the hotel scene with a sense of disgust and fury.

He let the girls disappear from view.

Let them have their fun.

He turned and headed away, as his fury morphed into a plan.

2

Detective Chief Inspector Paul Cullen of the British Transport Police stepped off the train at Wigan North Western railway station, gateway to his hometown, and looked along the platform. Sarah was waiting down near the small coffee shop, and the sight of his wife's smile as she spotted him lifted his spirits. He'd spent the two and a half hours from London Euston thinking about their current situation, wondering if his wife's decision to move back up north on a temporary basis was more than it seemed. But those doubts melted in their warm embrace.

She kissed him briefly but tenderly on the lips. 'I missed you.'

'Me too,' he replied.

It was only a week since she had travelled up to Wigan, but it had felt longer.

'You look tired,' Sarah said, as she gazed into his emerald green eyes.

'Thanks. You look good.'

She reached up his six foot three inch frame and nested

her fingers into his short, dark hair. 'Thank you, Detective, your powers of observation remain strong.'

They smiled at one another, before making their way down the stairs, hand in hand, to the car park.

'You want me to drive?' Cullen said. Sarah wasn't keen on being behind the wheel, so he usually did the driving.

'It's okay,' she said. 'I'm fine. You be the passenger for once.'

Cullen shrugged. In truth, he liked to be in control and was never good at letting someone else take the lead, whether that be motoring or otherwise. But he was tired after the journey.

'So, I haven't spoken to you properly about last week,' Sarah said, as she eased the car out of the car park and onto the main road.

'It was a long week,' he said, watching out of the window as they approached and passed the area around Wigan's famous pier. He'd spent many a summer's day down by that canal.

'Do you want to tell me about it?'

'Later,' he replied.

Sarah nodded, but wasn't prepared to let it go. 'I spoke to Amy about it,' she revealed. 'She tells me Natalie is doing okay.'

Natalie Long. Their daughter Amy's friend, and university housemate, who had been the focus of Paul Cullen's attention the previous week. Natalie had vanished in mysterious circumstances, and Paul (at Amy's request) had taken it upon himself to conduct an unofficial investigation into her disappearance.

'Yes, she's getting support from the local force over in Bristol.'

Thankfully the case had been resolved satisfactorily, but not without Paul jeopardising his career by going against orders from the Chief Superintendent.

'And you're okay?' Sarah glanced across. 'You're safe in your job?'

'For now.'

'I thought you said Maggie Ferguson was as unforgiving as she was formidable?'

'I did say something like that, didn't I?' he smiled mischievously.

'Maybe she has a soft spot for you,' Sarah teased.

'Maybe,' Paul teased back.

'Either that, or she knows an excellent DCI when she sees one, and she doesn't want to lose you.'

'She had every right to throw the book at me.'

'But instead she's given you the week off.'

'A non-negotiable week off. In Wigan.'

'Still...it's with me, so it can't be that bad.'

Cullen chuckled. He'd missed their banter the previous week.

Their discussion had diverted his attention, and only now did he realise that Sarah had not taken the usual turning towards her brother's house, the place where she was currently staying. They were now heading away.

Sarah seemed to notice that Cullen had realised something wasn't right, throwing a quick glance across at him.

'We're going to see Philip,' she said, pre-empting his question.

Cullen tensed. 'Can't we go back to the house first?'

'He's asking for you.'

Cullen was shocked. 'Asking for me? But he hasn't spoken in nearly twelve months.'

'He's been asking for you, Paul. As much as you might not want to, you need to see him, now.'

'So, he said my name?'

'I got a call from the carers, to tell me that Philip had spoken. He said the word "Paul".

'Are you sure?'

They were en route to Acorn House, the residential care home in the rural outskirts of the town, where Sarah's brother Philip had resided for the past two years. Four years ago, the sporty, strong rugby league playing Philip had been diagnosed with early-onset dementia.

'I dashed over there straight away,' Sarah explained, as she negotiated a roundabout, pulling out in front of a coach closer than Cullen would have liked. 'To be honest, I expected to be disappointed, that I'd get there and he would be silent again. At first, he was. I did wonder myself whether the carers had imagined it. But then I heard it for myself, crystal clear - he looked right at me and said "Paul". And the look he had, I just knew he was asking for you.'

'I can't believe it.'

The signs that something was seriously wrong with Philip had been there for a few years before - forgetting things, but putting it down to being busy. Then he couldn't remember names of even the closest of friends and relatives. A keen runner, he started to go missing for hours at a time, not taking his mobile, only to return without any recollection of where he had been. And most worryingly, he started leaving on the gas hob after cooking.

His deterioration had been spectacular and shocking.

Philip was the reason why Sarah had last week moved back up to their hometown of Wigan. Her brother's descent had accelerated, and he was in recent weeks becoming abusive to the carers in Acorn House.

And at six foot three, like Paul Cullen himself, he was not a man to be messed with.

There had been talk of possibly moving him out to a more secure environment, but Sarah was desperate to avoid that if at all possible. She had decided that more regular, daily contact with her might help to settle him down, maybe even improve his memory function, but at least keep his place in what was one of the best care homes for dementia in North West England.

'Are you okay?' Sarah asked, as they pulled up in a parking space at Acorn House.

Cullen nodded.

'You're mad at me, for forcing you to come here.'

Cullen shook his head. 'I'm mad at myself,' he admitted. 'For not coming here sooner.'

Sarah placed a hand on his. 'I understand, Paul. It's not easy, seeing your best friend the way he is.'

The guilt was like an uncomfortable lump in his throat. 'I should have been there for him.'

Sarah kept her hand in place. It felt warm and comforting, as was her kind smile. 'You're here now.'

3

Cullen and Sarah reported to reception, who informed them that Philip was in the main lounge and then they made their way up to the first floor. Acorn House was a modern, purpose built complex designed specifically for the needs of people with dementia. It followed the latest evidence, that placing people in environments that they felt comfortable in, and remembered, really helped.

For many of the residents, who were in their senior years, this meant references back to the 1960's and 1970's, which was why there was a juke box playing the Beatles' Ticket to Ride as they passed the nostalgically-styled cafe area. Several elderly residents were sitting hunched around tables draped with red and white checked linen, with cups of tea and biscuits on china plates.

'You okay?' Sarah asked.

Cullen nodded, but was uncharacteristically nervous.

He followed Sarah through towards the lounge, taking her lead through the building like a man walking to the gallows.

To his shame, it was only the second time he had been here in the years since Philip had arrived, so he didn't really know his way around.

The main lounge area was mocked up to resemble a private living room, with fireplace, mantelpiece, sofas and a large, flat-screen television over in the corner. Again, it was designed to put the residents at ease, to soothe their minds.

Philip was sitting bolt upright over on one of the individual chairs, looking blankly at the bay of windows, his large hands planted firmly on his knees.

'Hi, Philip,' Sarah said, as they approached. 'I've brought someone to see you.' She smiled lovingly and placed a kiss on his right cheek. 'Someone you've been asking about.'

Cullen moved into shot and watched for any sign of recognition. But Philip didn't flinch. He looked so out of place in many ways, this well-built, smartly dressed man in his mid-forties, surrounded by people who were nearly double his age. But in other ways, to Cullen's continued horror, he fitted right in. He was the shell of his best friend. A ghost.

Except that he wasn't a ghost - he was still Philip, living and breathing.

He was still the man Cullen had met over thirty years previously, on that first night of junior rugby training. The boy with the cheeky smile and sense of mischief to go with it. The boy who would soon introduce him to Sarah, the shy young little sister who would later become Cullen's childhood sweetheart.

'Philip,' Cullen said, 'how are things?'

It was a stupid question, and Cullen chastised himself for it.

How are things?!

But what else was he to say?

As a police officer, Cullen was a master of communication. He could chat as happily and easily with all walks of society; crooks and cops, victims and villains. And yet when it came to his poor, damaged best friend, he was at a loss for words.

As Cullen searched for the next sentence, Sarah pulled across chairs for them both.

'I'm sorry I haven't been to visit in a while, mate,' Cullen managed, as he took the seat. He gazed into Philip's eyes for some response, but the stare was unwavering, the eyes like they were unseeing. 'I'm really sorry,' Cullen added, emotion catching in his throat as he started to choke up.

I haven't been to visit because I'm scared.

But I've really wanted to see you, many times...

'I told Paul you've been asking for him,' Sarah prompted, touching the side of his arm. 'You've been saying his name, haven't you?'

Still no response.

Cullen looked over to Sarah in a silent request for guidance. She gestured for him to continue talking.

'You look well,' he said. Again, he regretted the words, lamenting his inability to communicate. The polite conversation, it just wasn't them. He remembered the banter that they would engage in down the pubs and clubs in the centre of town on a Thursday night. 'Actually, mate, to be honest, I've seen you looking better.'

Sarah glanced across, surprised at the sudden change of tone, but Cullen continued.

'I still remember that length of the field try you scored against Sydney Roosters, in the World Club Challenge, to win the game in the final minute. I think that was your career highlight, right?'

Philip had reached the top of rugby league, playing over three hundred times for the world famous Wigan Warriors, as a fearsome second row forward. He had devastating speed off the mark and could knock over the biggest of opponents.

Those hundreds of big hits, had it led to the dementia? It was a question they'd discussed with doctors at the time of Philip's diagnosis, but there was no definitive answer despite the growing evidence linking head injuries to degenerative brain disease.

Cullen had, selfishly he couldn't help feeling, pondered on more than one occasion whether this might be his future, given the fact that he had played the same game, taken similar hits, up until his early twenties.

'That try just blew me away, mate. I'll never forget it. Do you remember?'

The dementia came just a couple of years after Philip's retirement from the sport, and curtailed a promising coaching career, which had seen him take over as head of the youth team at Wigan.

'I'm sure you must remember it, don't you?'

Still Philip failed to respond.

'Deep in there, mate, in that head of yours, there must be something left, memories of it all, or some of it.'

Cullen felt a single tear escape and trickle down his face. Surprised, not known for displaying his emotions, he brushed it away with a manly hand.

Sarah watched on intently.

'You're still my best friend, Phil, and I'm sorry I haven't been to see you for so long, I'm so sorry.'

Just as Cullen thought that there would be nothing back, Philip turned his head towards him, and his mouth opened.

'Yes?' Cullen asked expectantly. 'You want to say something, mate?'

'You look like a kind man,' his best friend whispered.

Cullen bit down hard on his emotions and fled the room.

'I'M SORRY,' Sarah said, wrapping an arm around Cullen as he was sitting in the back office of Philip's house. Cullen had been in there for the past ten minutes, ever since they'd returned from the residential home.

He'd been looking at the walls. They were full of memories, times when his friend was at the height of his rugby league career. Photographs of Philip bursting through tackles, celebrating victories with overjoyed teammates, one of him diving over the try-line, the ball clamped safely under his arm, his face ablaze with delight.

'You've got no need to apologise,' Cullen said, turning with a sad smile. 'It should be me, saying sorry to you. And to Phil.'

Sarah shook her head. 'I shouldn't have pushed you into that. I should have let it happen in its own time, when you were ready.'

Cullen laughed. 'I don't think I'd ever have been ready. Then was as good a time as any. I just wish I'd handled it better.'

Cullen hadn't returned to the room after his swift departure. Sarah had come looking for him almost immediately, and they had decided it was best if they came back another day.

'It will get easier,' Sarah said. 'The more you see Philip, the easier it will get.'

Cullen searched her eyes. 'I'm not sure it will.'

'Talk to me about it,' she replied. 'Why do you find it so hard?'

Cullen looked around the room again, searching for the right words. They'd never properly talked about the situation, even when Sarah had announced that she was moving back up to Wigan to be near her brother. Cullen's unwillingness to visit, or even discuss Philip, had been an unspoken topic over the past two years.

'I thought it was because I was scared,' he said.

'Scared?'

'Scared that what's happening to Phil might also happen to me.'

'Because of the rugby?'

He nodded. That is something they had talked about, in those early days. 'I was also worried the same might happen to you.'

'Me?'

That was something he hadn't dared to discuss with Sarah before now. It had been just too frightening. 'We know it can run in families.'

'We can never know what fate has in store for us,' Sarah dismissed.

'I guess not.'

'You said you'd thought it was because you were scared,' she said. 'Is that not what you think now?'

'No,' he admitted. 'The real reason is worse than that.'

4

Olivia Byron stifled a yawn as she approached the building that housed the offices of Turn Around, the charity for young people where she had worked as an Engagement Officer for the past four years. The charity, small but active across the country, worked with the most vulnerable children, many of whom had come to the end of the line with formal education. It worked with local authorities to offer the vulnerable young people a new start, and a new chance. Something that they would never otherwise have got. She absolutely adored her job and loved coming to work.

But not so much today.

She had felt pretty awful from the moment she had woken, her head groggy from the previous night's birthday drinks in a cocktail bar just down from the cinema where she and the small group of friends had watched Sing-along Mamma Mia.

How she wished that she had resisted the temptation to have those last few bright blue shots that her friend and colleague Katherine had thrust into her hand towards the end of the night.

She pushed down her feelings of sickness, brought on by the short but painful trip through the revolving doors and practised her brightest, freshest smile on Linda at reception.

My goodness she needed a coffee.

Yawning again so wide that it made her jaw click, she made her way past the still-to-open book shop to the ground floor café and ordered her usual skinny flat white and poppy and lemon seed muffin, which she would try and save for her mid-morning snack.

'Good weekend?' Ruben asked behind the counter, as he took her re-useable cup and placed it under the coffee machine with practised efficiency.

Olivia wondered whether this was a reference to the way she looked.

Wow, you look like you've had a hard weekend...

'Your thirtieth,' the handsome New Zealander explained with a warm smile and the brownest of eyes. 'Did you have a good night out last night, for your birthday?'

She was just being paranoid. It wasn't about how she looked at all. Ruben was being his usual lovely self. 'Great night, thanks,' she replied. 'Perfect way to spend the special day.'

A thought flashed through Olivia's head, about how her birthday could have been made even more perfect, and she blushed at the fantasy.

'I missed you on the tube this morning,' Ruben added, turning to finish off making the coffee as another customer arrived and stood in line.

'Me too,' she said, blushing again.

Olivia had struck up a developing friendship with the

quiet but assured Ruben Wilkins over a period of weeks shortly after he had first started work at the café, two months ago. They bumped into each other on the tube one morning and realised that they shared the same commute, on the Northern Line from Edgware. Since then they had shared many journeys and got to know one another better.

'Well there's always tomorrow,' he added.

Ruben worked part time in the café, Mondays, Tuesdays and Wednesdays, while studying part-time for a doctorate in infectious disease management at the London School of Global Health. She missed the days he wasn't present behind the counter.

'There certainly is.'

And there was that smile and eye-contact again from him.

Was she just imaging the chemistry between them?

After all, Ruben was the kind of guy who was friendly and warm with everyone, so it would be easy to misread the signs. Olivia hadn't had the courage to ask him if he was in a relationship, but he'd never mentioned a partner. Single for the past two years, she harboured hopes that their friendly conversations might lead to something more. But being naturally shy and lacking confidence, Olivia wasn't the kind of girl who would make the first move.

'Well, I'd better be going,' was all she could manage, aware that the lady was still waiting in line behind her, and well within earshot.

'Have a great day,' Ruben replied. 'And see you tomorrow.'

Olivia savoured the warm goodbye and left reinvigorated with a spring in her step, heading for the stairs and the second floor.

Olivia gazed out at the busy traffic passing along Euston Road as she reached the second floor. The charity was lucky to have secured such a prime location for a relatively low rent, being hosted in the headquarters of the Future Earth Foundation, a global sustainability foundation that let out part of its building to a number of small charities. Each of the charities had their own part of a floor, and shared communal facilities like the lovely café and bookshop on the ground level.

It was a brilliant environment to work in.

'Hey, Olivia,' Katherine said, looking up from her computer screen with her desk covered with papers. It looked like she'd been in full flow for some time. Despite drinking just as much as her the previous night, she looked fresh and energetic.

Olivia didn't know how she managed it.

Olivia had learnt very quickly, in the first week of the job in fact, that Katherine not only liked to drink, but also had a remarkable ability to seem unaffected by it.

'Well,' Katherine continued, 'I must admit, I did wonder whether you'd actually be in at all today. Fair play, you look pretty rough, if you don't mind me saying.'

Katherine's mischievous smile softened the blow. Katherine, a trained teacher, was the education lead for the charity, being responsible for organising programs of activity for the young people, including residential courses which they put on in association with a network of outward-bound centres across the country. She was such an enthusiastic and talented person, and always managed to get the best out of the people with whom she worked, including not just the young people themselves, but also her colleagues.

'Sorry I had to go early,' the redhead girl said from over

the other side of the office. Heather, who at twenty-three was the youngest of the team, was the charity's administrative officer. She also acted as self-taught web designer and social media guru. 'Katherine said I missed the main action.'

'The karaoke,' Olivia said, thinking back to the slightly cringe worthy moment when she and her friends had screamed out the words to Abba's Dancing Queen for a thankfully almost empty bar.

'It was epic,' Katherine commented. 'Pity we haven't got any video.'

'Yeah, pity,' Olivia said sarcastically.

'I really can't stand karaoke,' Henry said, not looking up from his screen. Henry, the only boy in the office, and at thirty-five the oldest of the team (apart from the boss Christina, who was in her mid 40s), was the financial controller. A trained accountant, he had worked for the charity for five years, after just under a decade with one of the big accountancy firms in the city.

'People who can't sing really shouldn't sing,' he continued. He looked up, processing what he had just said. 'I didn't mean...'

Henry was an acquired taste, with a wit as dry as the Sahara, and on first or even second or third meeting could put people off with his slightly off-centre manner and worldview. But he was in fact a lovely guy once you got to know and understand him.

'It's okay, Henry,' Olivia replied. 'You're right.'

Henry nodded, validated. 'I'm sorry, I meant to send a card,' he said.

'Oh, don't worry,' Olivia replied, but Henry was already back to work with his eyes fixed on the computer screen.

THE DAY PASSED SLOWLY and painfully for Olivia, as she struggled to shake off the hangover from the previous night. The sickness had gone thankfully, but the tiredness refused to budge. In a desperate effort to energise herself, she overdosed on peppermint tea, wolfed down the muffin that she had purchased earlier and then demolished an overly large pasta meal from the nearby Pret A Manger. In a further effort to stay alert, she plugged herself in to an upbeat dance playlist and turned up the volume, pumping out Balearic beats that did stop her from falling asleep at her desk, but made it almost impossible to concentrate.

Fortunately, she had just one phone call scheduled, to a small production company who they had commissioned to produce a short video promoting the work of the charity. It was in the latter stages of development, and the call was to agree the key lines that would go with the visuals.

Although she'd been dreading the call, given the way she was feeling, it actually galvanised her, and the rest of the afternoon went better. She managed to clear her emails and plan out tasks for the next day.

Her focus had returned so much that she was surprised by the appearance of someone at her shoulder.

'These arrived for you,' Heather said, handing over a large bunch of flowers. 'A courier just dropped them off at reception.'

Olivia cradled the flowers and picked out the note:

Sorry for being late with these. Hope you had an ABBA-solutely fantastic birthday!

'Lovely flowers,' Katherine commented, as Olivia was still reading the message. 'Who are they from?'

Katherine was never backward in coming forward.

'It doesn't say,' Olivia said. She was a bit uncomfortable with the attention and was glad that Henry had headed out of the office for a meeting thirty minutes earlier.

Olivia admired the lovely mix of roses and orchids. It must have been an expensive selection.

'Oooh, *mysterious!*' Katherine exclaimed. 'Maybe a secret admirer?'

'Probably my mum,' Olivia replied, although in truth she really doubted it. Her mum wasn't a flowers person.

She tried to rein in her excitement at the thought of who might have actually sent them.

Could they be from Ruben?

She really hoped so.

5

There was one thing that Detective Constable Tony Beswick hated more than shopping.

And that was shopping for his wife.

Brenda's fiftieth birthday was on Tuesday. Today was Monday. He'd deliberately left it late, to shorten the duration of the pain. But now, as he tramped around the stores of Oxford Street, he was beginning to regret his tardiness.

He was sure she'd mentioned something a few months' ago that she was keen to have...clothing? Jewellery?

He couldn't for the life of him remember.

As he stood on the ground floor of the John Lewis department store, surrounded by items that may or may not have been suitable, he felt like screaming.

It wasn't that Brenda was difficult to buy for. He would have been the same with anyone. When it came to present buying, he had zero imagination and zero empathy.

It was such a painful experience.

The only good thing about this misadventure, now

nearing three hours, was that it had taken his mind off the dull chest pain he'd been bothered by since early morning.

Probably indigestion...

'Can I help you, Sir?' one of the assistants asked him, with what sounded like a note of pity. She was probably well-used to coming to the aid of hapless men who were floundering in the aisles, all with that same pained expression.

'I wish,' Tony replied. 'I'm shopping for my wife's fiftieth.'

She nodded, seemingly up for the challenge. 'Does your wife have a favourite perfume?'

'Not sure,' he replied, slightly embarrassed.

'We have a wide range,' she said, undeterred. 'All the major brands.' She led him over to a nearby counter. 'This is new in this month. Been very popular among ladies of a certain age. I can say that, because I'm in that category,' she laughed.

She sprayed the perfume onto a small piece of card and handed it to him. He took a sniff.

Whoa!

'Not to your taste?' she enquired.

He let out a rasping cough. 'No...not...too much.'

The smell was so pungent, it would probably knock down flies.

'Maybe another one then, a more subtle fragrance.' She moved across to another table as he followed obediently, like a dog hoping for a treat from their master.

'This is probably more to your liking,' she proclaimed with what Tony felt sure would prove to be misplaced confidence. 'If you're not used to those strong bouquets...'

Flowers? What did bouquets have to do with it?

'...Then it's likely your wife wears something more delicate, something like this.'

Again, she sprayed a card and handed it to him.

With more than a little reticence, he sniffed at the card.

He could hardly smell anything.

Maybe the spray nozzle hadn't worked. Although he was sure he had seen the mist.

He looked at the bottle.

'How much is it?'

Her face brightened. 'This one? Sixty-five pounds.'

He gulped.

'But you do get a complimentary travel bag,' she added, gesturing to the sparkly gold bag at the counter.

Tony wasn't sure it was Brenda's style. He couldn't remember whether she had use for such bags.

But he was looking for a container for his spare nuts and bolts. Maybe that would fit the bill.

How much was he willing to pay to end this day, here and now?

But sixty five pounds...

'I'm sure your wife will love it.'

Tony wasn't so sure. He wasn't even confident that Brenda actually wore perfume, now he came to think about it.

'I'll take it.'

HE FELT the ache again at the till point, just as he was reaching for his wallet.

Could be a pulled muscle...

He shook off the fears that he had left unvoiced that morning, and paid for the perfume, which the assistant had gift-wrapped beautifully.

All he had to do was write a message on the tag.

And get a birthday card...

He'd forgotten about the card!

That would surely be an easier task. Although even with that, there were a lot of decisions to be made - funny or serious, age specific or not, glitter or no glitter, maybe one with a badge?

Too much choice!

The ache pulsed again as he made his way back out onto Oxford Street. There must be plenty of card shops. And there was always WH Smiths.

He could pick up a snack there too. Maybe his favourite - Cadbury's with hazelnut.

Although he really shouldn't. He'd promised Brenda, himself, and Paul that he would try and lose a few pounds.

But one little bar couldn't hurt.

He was still thinking of that chocolate bar when he heard the shout.

'Hey, he's got my bag!'

Tony turned just as a young boy came sprinting towards him. It was just too soon to be able to react, and the youth, bag in hand, flashed past him with a super reactive side-step.

The lady came next, with a miserable effort to retrieve the stolen property. She could hardly move past walking pace and stopped before she got past the off-duty officer.

'Don't worry,' Tony found himself saying to her, 'I'm police. Stay here. I'll get your bag back.'

He turned and set off after the boy, forgetting for a minute that he was carrying the perfume, which swung hard against his knee.

He dodged and weaved through the shoppers, trying to keep his target in sight.

But the youth had already gone.

And he felt awful. There was no way he was going to catch him. His pulse throbbed in his neck, and his left arm ached terribly.

He slowed to a stop and reached out for the nearby bus stop, panting.

'You okay?' someone asked from the queue.

'I...think...so,' he managed, now gasping for breath.

But even as he said it, it sounded ludicrous.

Surely, he wasn't that out of shape?

He'd run for a matter of metres, and now he couldn't breathe...

'You don't look okay,' the person pressed. 'Maybe you need an ambulance?'

Tony actually laughed through the pain and shook his head.

'I'm just a little...'

And then he slumped to the ground.

6

The call came through just before eight on the Monday evening. Cullen was settled on the sofa with Sarah, her feet tucked up beside him, as they watched one of the popular cookery programmes.

After the previous week, it was good to enjoy a bit of normality, and being back with Sarah - even if it was in someone else's home - felt amazing and right.

'I'm sorry things have been so difficult,' he said, as he stroked a hand up and down her back. 'I feel like I haven't done enough recently.'

She raised her head. 'It's been hard for you too. With Amy especially.'

They had supported their daughter Amy through a traumatic period over the past few years. Indeed, Amy's intense and deep battles with the anxiety that had attacked her during the final years of her schooling, leading her to the brink of self-destruction, had tested Cullen and Sarah's marriage to its limit. And it had taken a longer-term toll on their relationship.

How could it not?

'I could have handled it better,' he admitted.

'Maybe. But then again, so could I.'

Their deep love for Amy had stirred strong emotions and reactions when it came to how to help her. They had fought. They had pushed one another away at times. And even though Amy was now in a much better place, the wounds to Cullen and Sarah's marriage were still healing.

'Look,' Sarah said, shifting to a proper sitting position and facing Cullen head on. 'We've all been through a lot. But we're still together.' She smiled. 'This could have broken us, but it hasn't. So now we move on and get on with the rest of our lives.'

Cullen nodded. He hesitated before saying what he instinctively wanted to say, wondering whether it was wise to bring this up. But it felt like the right time to finally clear the air. 'My job,' he said. 'The move to London. I know that's been part of the problem. Maybe a larger part than we want to admit.'

Sarah too caught herself before reacting. She seemed more reticent to engage with this now but decided too it was time.

'It has been hard,' she admitted. She smiled sadly. 'Harder than I ever expected.'

Cullen nodded. He couldn't believe really that in the years since they had moved down from the North West to the South East, they had never had this conversation. It had been an unspoken, assumed issue, but not one that had ever reached the top of their priority list, given what they had had to deal with in helping their daughter.

The fact that they could now discuss it must surely be a good sign.

'I'm sorry,' he said. And he was sorry. He knew that Sarah would never have chosen to leave her home region if he hadn't been so keen to go for the London-based role with the British Transport Police. The move had all been for him.

'You don't need to apologise for anything.'

'I know you didn't really want to move.'

She shrugged.

'I can try and get a move back,' he heard himself saying, much to his own surprise. 'I can see if I can relocate to the Leeds office. It's commutable from here.'

'You don't need to do that.'

'I will though.' Although his stomach sank as he spoke the words. He loved his job in the capital. It had been everything he had hoped for and more. The thought of giving that up left him feeling sick.

But the offer he had just made was genuine. He would give it all up if it made a difference.

The job was important, but his marriage was everything.

'I appreciate what you're saying, Paul, I really do. But honestly, I'm fine.'

Cullen wasn't sure. 'Ideally, you'd rather be living up here.'

'Yes,' was the immediate reply. 'Of course. This is my home, the place where we grew up, my friends and family are still here. It's familiar. And comforting.'

'I will quit London,' he assured her.

'I don't want you to. Life is about trade-offs, about compromise. And for now, it's the compromise. But maybe one day, we will move back...'

Cullen looked troubled.

'I need to make more of an effort,' Sarah continued, taking his hand. 'I need to want to make it work. Up until now, I just haven't had the will or desire to try - I couldn't think of anything else apart from Amy...and Philip.'

'It's understandable.'

Sarah also had her job. She was a primary school teacher.

'But now we're through that, we can make things better. I can try harder.'

They embraced.

Only to be interrupted by Cullen's phone as it burst to life.

He nearly let it ring off, but Sarah pulled back for him to answer.

It was a London number, coming from British Transport Police Headquarters.

'Paul Cullen.'

'Paul.' It was Maggie Ferguson, the Chief Superintendent, his fearsome boss. The woman who had ordered him to have his week of rest. The woman who had threatened to end his career following his off-duty investigation the previous week.

He stood up without thinking, already on alert for what was to come.

'I've got some bad news,' she stated, soberly. 'About DS Beswick.'

~

'WHAT'S HAPPENED?'

Sarah had already risen from the sofa, as the seriousness of the call, revealed by Cullen's ashen face, began to register.

'It's Tony. He's suffered a heart attack. Earlier today. Was rushed to Barts.'

He held the phone limply by his side, thinking through his options. DS Beswick was a close colleague and friend. They'd been close ever since Cullen had arrived in the capital from Manchester and the two men had worked as a tight-knit investigating duo on countless investigations.

Serious investigations that left their mark.

And those kinds of experiences bring people together.

'Is it okay?' she asked with genuine concern. Sarah knew Tony and his wife, Brenda, well too. They had been out for meals a number of times and had holidayed together the previous year in Brighton.

'I'm not sure,' Cullen replied. 'He collapsed in the street and they rushed him in for emergency angioplasty.'

The process of putting tiny stents - metal tubes - into blocked or collapsed arteries to force them open, was familiar to them both. Sarah's father had undergone the same procedure five years ago, and it had saved his life.

'But you don't know whether it's been successful?' Sarah asked.

Cullen shook his head. 'Maggie said the last update was that he was being taken into theatre. They don't know the outcome. Poor Brenda.' He ran a hand across his face.

'You need to be with him,' Sarah said, stealing his thoughts.

'You think I should go now? What about...'

'Philip will be here waiting for you,' she said, again reading him with ease. It was one of the things he loved about her - usually he prided himself on his ability to shield his thoughts, from suspects and colleagues - but she got him every time.

Almost every time.

'I can come back up here later this week,' he said, thinking out loud.

'Of course, you can,' Sarah reassured him. 'But for now, Tony and Brenda need you.'

'Thanks.'

'But promise me one thing, Paul.'

'Yes?'

'You'll wait until the morning. It's too late for the train, and I don't want you driving down at night. Not with all this on your mind.'

7

Ruben was waiting by the bench on the platform, as Olivia approached. He looked up and smiled, shielding his eyes against the early morning sunshine.

'Hey,' he said. 'Lovely morning.'

'Yes,' Olivia agreed. 'Beautiful.'

'I see you've got your morning gossip fix ready,' he commented, gesturing towards the newspaper that was tucked under her arm. She was an avid reader of the London Daily Post, and its often-silly celebrity stories helped to while away the commute.

'Sure have,' feeling ever so slightly embarrassed with her love of the paper. It was pretty trashy, she had to admit, and it was notable that despite the paper being available free of charge in vast numbers in and around the transport network, she'd never once seen Ruben with a copy in hand.

He'd been too polite to make any pointed remarks about the paper to her, but it didn't take much interpretation to detect the sense of disapproval he felt, apparent through the thinly veiled friendly banter.

Olivia glanced across to see what Ruben was reading. He was part-way through the book.

'It's my current favourite read,' Ruben said, noticing Olivia's interest. 'It's about how capitalists profit from global shocks,' he explained. 'You know, it's just so frustrating, the more you find out about what's really going on in this world.'

Ruben was somewhat of an activist; Olivia knew that from the past conversations. He was an active member of a climate change protest group and had demonstrated with friends just last week on a big march in Trafalgar Square. He was also very much into social justice, which wasn't surprising given the topic of his doctoral studies. Olivia really admired his sense of justice, even though she could never take it to the extremes that he evidently did. Ruben had actually been arrested the previous year, one of a number of protesters who had glued themselves to the front entrance of UGT, the multinational investment bank who it is alleged had close ties with unscrupulous mining corporations that had exploited villagers in South America.

'You can borrow it after I finished, if you like,' he offered. 'I think you'll find it shocking and eye-opening; people need to know what's going on.'

Olivia nodded, gazing at the handsome man next to her, wondering whether all that passion for social justice, all that desire to solve the world's most difficult problems was just too much to bear really. Of course, she herself shared his concerns, but it just seemed such a big task; surely it could be enough to drive someone crazy when they really didn't have the power to change what was going on at that global level.

'We can make a difference,' Ruben said suddenly, as if reading her mind. 'We can affect change, we can choose to take a new path, so the future is better for ourselves, our children and our children's children.'

Olivia could see that he really believed that, and she felt bad for her lack of ambition when faced with Ruben's passion.

Maybe Ruben, and those like him would be able to change the world.

The train filled during the next few minutes, before the doors slid shut and it moved off southbound. After a few minutes of polite conversation, they both settled into their respective reads. As Olivia perused the news and gossip offered up by the London Daily Post, she felt quite inadequate when glancing over at Ruben's intense concentration on his worthy book. She didn't like to interrupt him, even though she was keen to strike up another conversation - this time about the flowers, and whether he was the sender. But she was desperate to know, and the longer she left it without asking, the weirder bringing up the issue would feel.

'Ruben,' Olivia said, deciding to finally take the plunge, 'I was wondering, was it you who sent the flowers?' She cursed herself at how nervous her voice sounded when she asked the question. She felt like an uncomfortable teenager again, plucking up the courage to speak to a boy in the school playground.

'Flowers?' Ruben replied, looking confused.

Olivia felt both embarrassed and crestfallen. It hadn't been him after all. She wished that she had just kept quiet, but now that she started it felt impossible to end the conversation.

'I received a bunch of flowers on Monday afternoon, for my birthday. They were really lovely, but it didn't say who they were from. I just thought, you know, after our conversation, that they might be from...you.'

Her eyes were pulled down to the floor as if heavy weights had been hung from her lids. She felt much more embarrassed than she should've done.

And then suddenly Ruben smiled. 'Oh, those flowers, yes they were from me. I hope you liked them, I wasn't sure whether you were into flowers or not.'

Olivia looked up at him and met his smile with hers. Suddenly the mood on this packed, otherwise joyless tube carriage, had been transformed. For a moment it felt like they were the only ones there.

'They were really lovely,' she said. 'In fact, they are actually my favourite type of flowers. I've got them up on my kitchen table. That was such a kind thing to do, thank you.'

'Don't mention it,' he said, 'It was my pleasure. I'm just sorry they were after the event.'

'You really don't need to be sorry.'

'That's good. But I was wondering, if there's something else I can do to make up for forgetting your birthday.'

'Yes?' Olivia tried her best to dampen any expectation of what Ruben was about to say.

'You know the Duck and Dog?'

'The pub?' It was just down the road from her flat, and she'd been there a few times with friends, but not for quite a while.

'Yes. They've got an open mike tonight, and I'm planning on doing a couple of songs.'

'You sing?'

Ruben nodded. 'Guitar mainly, but yes I do try,' he said. 'Would you like to come along? We can have a drink and you can let me know how terrible you think my performance is.'

'I'd love to come,' Olivia said, beaming. 'And I'm sure your performance will be fantastic.'

'That's brilliant,' he said. 'It's a date.'

They both settled back into reading, although Olivia wasn't really taking in any of the articles from the newspaper. She was just too excited to concentrate.

A date!

Ruben referred to it as a date. She couldn't quite believe how well this had gone and was already nervous and super excited about the evening. She wondered how she was going to concentrate at work waiting for the night out.

8

Sarah dropped Cullen off at the station just after eight in the morning and he caught the train direct back to London Euston. He spent the journey thinking about his friend DS Beswick and how he was doing. He'd phoned Tony's wife, Brenda, to let her know he was coming, and she seemed very appreciative of the support, if a little embarrassed that Cullen was putting himself out so much.

But that was his call.

Cullen also used the journey to think about Philip again, and how he reacted upon seeing his best friend. He still couldn't help thinking about how terrible the situation was and how helpless it made him feel. He still felt guilty about running out the way he did and wondered whether Philip was aware of anything that was going on.

Have you been sitting there in the chair outwardly not saying anything but inwardly aware of everything?

The train pulled into Euston just after ten and he headed straight for the tube. Cullen knew the network in London like the back of his hand; once a stranger to the city he'd spent many hours underground both on and off business. When he was younger, as a dyed in the wool Northerner, he'd never dreamt that not only would he come to work in London, but just how much he would enjoy it. The thrills of the big city, the sheer number of people, the movement, the danger, the variety. It made him feel alive and got the adrenaline coursing through his veins.

Cullen emerged from the tube, heading towards the hospital where his friend was being treated. He still knew nothing of his condition overnight and suddenly felt fearful about what might come and what he might find. Approaching the reception desk, he had second thoughts about whether it was good to just turn up without warning.

After all, he wasn't family.

But the person on the reception desk was happy to direct him up to the fourth floor. His nerves grew as the lift opened and he stepped out, walking up towards the nursing station, wondering what state Tony was in.

'Hello can I help you?' the nurse asked from behind the desk, looking up from her paperwork.

'I was hoping to see Tony Beswick,' Cullen said. 'I'm a friend.'

She looked across at the computer, tapped a couple of things and then said, 'he's in recovery. You're welcome to see him, but he might not be up for much conversation - he'll be drowsy for a while yet until the drugs wear off.'

Cullen entered the recovery area, which consisted of a number of individual rooms off the main corridor. Beswick's name was on the first door on the left.

The door was slightly ajar but Cullen paused as his hand touched the frame. Preparing himself for the sight to come, he slowly pushed the door open and stepped into the room. Tony was lying on the bed, hooked up to various pieces of hospital apparatus. He was sleeping soundly. He looked totally washed out, his face ashen, and not at all like his usual ruddy complexion. It was quite a shock. Although Beswick was in no way the fittest and healthiest officer in ranks of the British Transport Police, he always had a kind of vitality that belied his frame. He was usually full of life and his face full of colour. But not at the moment.

Cullen pulled across a chair from the side as he sat down at a comfortable distance, not wanting to intrude on his sleeping friend.

He would stay for a few minutes.

But unbelievably, as if Tony could sense his colleague in the room, he began to stir. His eyes opened slowly and his head turned towards the visitor. At first he seemed confused about who he was looking at, but then quickly recognition hit and he even managed to smile.

'Boss,' he said. 'How did you..'

'Maggie Ferguson,' Cullen replied. 'She called last night, told me the news.'

Beswick seemed almost not to listen to Cullen's reply, his mind probably floating somewhere other than the place where he lay. 'I'm honoured,' he said finally.

'You look...better than I expected,' Cullen said.

This brought a smile from Tony, although it was through a grimace of sorts. 'You were in Wigan,' he said, 'with Sarah. You came back here when you heard the news?' Tony gazed at him with drugged-up eyes.

'I had to,' Cullen replied. 'I just had to come as soon as I heard. You would do the same for me,' he added. 'Anyway, I got Sarah's blessing. She wanted me to come back and support you and Brenda. To be here for you both.'

'It's great to see you, Paul. Thank you.'

9

'I'm really glad to see you,' Tony said, looking at Cullen with watery-weak eyes. 'At least I know I've not died and gone to heaven, with you standing in front of me,' he joked.

Cullen laughed along with him. 'You're damn right' he said. 'If this was your heaven, this room would have a dart-board, one hundred percent.'

'Seriously though, Boss, I'm so glad to see you. I mean, yesterday, was so scary. I just didn't know whether I was going to make it. I just felt so out of it, everything was like a dream, a bad dream, I just felt like I was slipping away you know.'

Cullen moved towards his friend and placed a hand on his hand. He searched for the right words, thinking back to the previous day when he had not known what to say to his friend Philip. Then he had come up short, very short. But now there was a chance to make things right. He just had to find the right words this time. He took a deep breath. 'You're going to be okay,' he said, 'you've got through the worst part. Brenda will be with you and I'll be here too. You're going to be okay,' he repeated.

Beswick gazed at him, seemingly lost for words. He opened his mouth as if to speak but then checked himself. There was something in the way Tony looked at him, the look of something that he couldn't quite put his finger on - was it that look of guilt, that Cullen had seen thousands of times before in the eyes of offenders?

But why?

'I've been so stupid, Boss,' Beswick said at last. 'I've just been so very, very stupid.'

'Everything is going to be okay,' Cullen said, wondering why his friend seemed so troubled. Maybe it was just the drugs talking; he knew sedatives could do this kind of thing. Maybe Beswick wasn't even thinking straight.

'I could've died,' Tony said, as a tear appeared from his eye and slipped down his cheek, quickly followed by another in the other eye. With both his arms connected to the equipment, he couldn't wipe away the tears as they fell, and they trickled down his neck under his chin.

'It's okay,' Cullen said, 'you're going to be fine, you're not going to die.'

Beswick shook his head. 'But I *could've* died,' he said. 'And it would've been all my fault.'

'No it wouldn't, it's not your fault. These things happen, you weren't to know.'

'I don't know if I will be able to face Brenda,' Beswick said. 'I just don't know how I'm going to be able to face her and look her in the eyes.'

'I don't know what you mean,' Cullen replied. 'I think you just need to rest.' He patted his friend on the arm.

'I can't see her,' he said, 'I just can't. Not after what I've done.'

'What do you mean?'

'I had lots of warnings,' he said. 'For the past few months I've known something was wrong; I was getting out of breath, you know, just walking down the street, walking upstairs - it was getting so difficult and then the pain in my chest, not all the time, but sometimes. And then more often the pain it was going down my arm. I thought I knew what it was, but I ignored it, because I was scared. I didn't tell Brenda. I was stupid.'

'Don't be too hard on yourself,' Cullen said. 'You weren't to know this would happen.' As Tony didn't look convinced, Cullen pressed home his point. 'I know how you feel, I know you feel guilty, but really you shouldn't. We need to focus on what's important. Getting better for Brenda and for us.'

~

CULLEN THOUGHT back to the past few weeks and whether there had been any signs that Tony had been unwell.

Had there been something that he'd missed?

Some sign that his heart had been on the edge of the attack?

There was the one thing. A day a few weeks ago when Tony had stopped short in the centre of London to catch his breath. He'd placed his hand on the nearby lamppost, to have a breather, and Cullen had joked that he needed to address his fitness.

But Tony had never been the fittest of police officers. In the years that Cullen had known him, he had never been anything like what you might call athletic. And he was getting on now in his mid fifties so the middle-age spread hadn't particularly seemed anything to worry about.

But now, Cullen did wonder why he had missed opportunities to counsel his friend to address some of his health issues. After all Cullen himself, a former rugby league player, still looked after himself physically. He played five-a-side football in the force league every week, and also took to the pool weekly. He felt as fit as he had done twenty years ago, even though he knew, approaching his mid forties, that time was not necessarily on his side.

He could've invited Tony to the football. Or recommended that he joined the gym or something. But looking at Tony in the bed, he knew that the suggestion would've gone down like a lead balloon. And Tony's health wasn't exactly his responsibility.

Or was it?

'Boss,' Tony said, gazing at Cullen as he was lost in thought. 'Don't look so worried, you're making me anxious. The doctors haven't said anything to you have they?'

'No, not at all,' Cullen replied. 'I know as much as you, don't worry, I was just thinking about how it could've been so much worse. It would've been terrible to lose you, mate.'

'I'm not going anywhere,' Tony said. He patted his chest. Not with these little babies inside me. They've put these metal tubes into my arteries, to keep them open. It's like scaffolding, they're so small, they got them in somehow, I don't really understand it. The doctor tried to explain, but I must admit I was a bit spaced out, and I didn't really understand what the guy was saying. It's still all a bit of a blur,' he added. He put his head back and closed his eyes for a moment and Cullen wondered whether he was just going to fall asleep there and then. But then he seemed to raise himself again and sat himself up a bit straighter in the bed.

'Boss,' he said. 'Can you do me a favour?'

'Of course,' Cullen replied, 'whatever you want.'

'You might regret saying that when you hear what the favour actually is.'

'Go on,' Paul said, now feeling slightly nervous about what the request was going to be, and how he could potentially refuse, if it was too strange an ask.

'Today is Brenda's birthday,' Tony revealed. 'She'll probably kill me for telling you this, but it's her fiftieth. And I've bought her tickets for a show, tonight.'

Cullen groaned inwardly, suddenly knowing what Beswick was about to ask of him. But somehow, he managed to keep a poker face as his friend continued.

'I've got tickets for Cats,' Tony said. 'It's her favourite show, she absolutely *loves* it, watched it about five times, but still she can't get enough of it. Obviously...' he said looking at Cullen for a reaction but not receiving one.

Not Cats!

'...I can't go with her,' Tony continued, 'but I wondered whether, you know, I know you don't like musicals but, I just wondered.'

Cullen decided to put his friend out of his misery. 'You want me to go with her,' he said.

'Yes, if you wouldn't mind, that would be brilliant, I would really appreciate it, it would make such a difference, and I wouldn't feel like such an idiot for ruining the day for her.'

'Sure, that won't be a problem,' Cullen replied.

How could he refuse?

Although he really did hate musical theatre. He hated it with a passion.

'Well,' Beswick said, looking slightly surprised as well as

very happy, 'that's wonderful, thank you so much, it really means a lot to me. And I know it will mean a lot to Brenda to.' He grimaced as he shifted in the bed.

Cullen struggled, but just succeeded in hiding his discomfort at the thought of spending an evening at the theatre. He would much rather have a quiet night in at the hotel, watch some television, crack open a beer. But this was his duty, to his friend, and he was more than happy to do it.

'Thanks so much,' Beswick said again, 'you know, I wasn't sure you'd say yes.'

The look on his face was worth the pain that would come. Sarah was also a fan of musicals, and throughout the years she had tried to convert Cullen to the artform, but had never succeeded. It was his idea of torture, seeing hyperactive performers jazz-handing it through three hours of what some saw as entertainment.

Give him a rugby field any day, two sides colliding with passion and intensity - that was his idea of entertainment.

'I know how much you hate that kind of thing,' Tony added. 'So do I.'

'Are you sure you haven't planned this heart attack?' Cullen said mischievously, 'to get out of having to go to the theatre?'

'I don't hate it that much,' Tony said, coughing. 'But now you say it, they have got the West Ham, Liverpool game on this evening,' he gestured to the TV console suspended to the left of the bed.

'Well, think of me,' Cullen replied, 'when you're enjoying the football.'

'I owe you one,' Beswick said.

'More than one,' Cullen quipped. 'Cats is my least favourite production of the lot. Saw it once with Sarah, and had to spend the second half of the performance feigning stomach ache so I could escape to the bar.'

~

Just a few minutes after Cullen had agreed to Tony's request to accompany Brenda to the theatre, she arrived at the hospital.

'Thanks so much, Paul,' she said outside in the corridor, after she had greeted her husband with a tender embrace. 'Tony told me about the theatre, and that you'll come with me. I'm not really sure I feel like going, with Tony the way he is, but he is insisting. It will make me feel a lot better if you could come with me. Because I know it will make Tony happy.'

'I'd be delighted to,' Cullen replied, this time actually meaning what he said.

'Do you think Tony is going to be okay?' Brenda said, in a hushed tone. She glanced back over her shoulder through the window, looking at her husband lying on the bed.

'I hope so,' Cullen replied. It was all you could say really, after all, he was a police officer, not a doctor. But he understood the need for reassurance from those close.

'I was just so worried,' she revealed, her eyes watery. 'When the call came through, I just thought, that was it. You know, as the wife of a police officer, I've always been afraid of that call, that knock on the door, to tell me the worst. To tell me that, you know...'

'I know,' Cullen replied. Sarah had said the same to him, just one time, a few years ago. The revelation of just how psychologically difficult it was being married to someone in the force, had actually shocked him. Maybe it was because he was so immersed in the job, comfortable with the risks, they hadn't really thought about the toll that it might take on the ones who were left wondering whether their loved one would come home at the end of the day.

And although Sarah had never mentioned the issue again, Cullen has never forgotten it.

'The Chief Superintendent called me,' she continued. 'I mean, it was really nice of her to do that, I really appreciate it, I really do, but you know, it just scares me so, so much...'

Cullen found himself bringing an arm around her shoulder and holding her as she started to sob. He looked over towards Tony, who thankfully was facing away, unaware of how his wife was suffering. 'It's going to be okay, Brenda, I promise. Everything is going to be okay.'

'I've tried to convince him to retire,' she said sniffing. 'You know that I retired last year, don't you? Well, I wanted Tony to do the same. I've always wanted to go on a cruise, you know, a big one. Maybe around the Mediterranean or even across the Atlantic. But, you know what Tony is like with the job, it's more than a job to him, he just says that he'll do it for one more year, but I'm just not sure he'll ever be ready to give it up.'

'Do you want me to say something?' Cullen said. 'As much as I don't want to see him go, I could have a word.'

'It's okay,' she said. 'Maybe after this, he'll have a think about what he wants to do with the rest of his life, now that he's had a second chance.'

'Sure.'

'You can stay at mine this evening, if you like,' she said. 'That came out sounding a bit wrong,' she said, actually blushing.

To his embarrassment, he felt his face redden also.

'Thanks for the offer, that's very kind, but I've booked the Excelsior, near Euston. It's good to be near the station, as I'm going to get the earliest train possible back up to Wigan, to be with Sarah and Philip.'

'Of course,' she replied, 'but if you change your mind, the offer is there.'

'Much appreciated.' Cullen looked at his watch, I think I'll head off now if that's okay with you. But if there's anything, just let me know, and I'll be back over straight away.'

Cullen said his goodbyes with Tony and Brenda, and arranged a place to meet later that evening for the show. Then he headed off to check-in at the hotel, after which he would then travel to his second home, British Transport Police Headquarters in Camden. He wasn't supposed to be working, but he just couldn't resist the urge to join the important meeting that was scheduled to take place in just under an hour's time.

10

He saw the girl on the platform at Liverpool Street station. She was tall, leggy, with a short skirt that circled a small waist. She looked Scandinavian, maybe Swedish, with her long blonde hair and glacial blue eyes.

As with most people these days, her attention was on her phone, probably scrolling through her inane Instagram feed, full of landscapes and people showing off about their wonderful lives.

The thought made him sweat. He could feel the wetness rise around the top of his neck and tingle in the heat of the underground.

The girl was standing just behind the yellow line, on her own. He took up a place a few feet away, gazing at her, forgetting about the CCTV cameras that watched down on them.

He felt empowered to do whatever he wanted. Up there, at ground level, they might have the upper hand, but down here, in the depths, he was powerful and unseen.

He could do whatever he wanted.

To think how many months he had wasted, tempering his

desires because of fear, when in fact he had nothing to fear at all.

Operation Archangel had not been able to touch him.

He moved even closer to the girl, not too close as to arouse her suspicion, but close enough to push her under the tube train as it rushed into the station.

But he wasn't planning to do such a thing.

Not now.

Even though he felt he could do it. A large part of him wanted to do it. His friends online had dared him to do it, to act out the fantasy that he had revealed. And now the curtain between reality and dark fantasy had been torn down, the possibilities staring him in the face were almost irresistible.

Almost.

So when the train heading westbound emerged, he simply followed the stunning yet annoying girl onto the carriage. He was pleased to find it was so busy that he could take up a position right behind her without alerting anyone as to his intentions.

It would make what he planned to do so, so easy.

HE WAS SO close to the girl that he could smell her shampoo, all fruity and fresh.

How he longed to bury his face in those golden strands, taking in her scent.

Before wrapping his fist around her hair and yanking hard and sudden, throwing her off her feet and dumping her on the dirt-ridden carriage floor.

She was still looking at her phone. He could see her playing one of those inane games that so many people on the tube - particularly girls - chose as their pastime. You had to line up jewels that were falling from above, before the screen filled.

He'd never played the game himself, but had spent more time than he cared to remember watching other people, so he knew exactly how it worked.

Pointless!

Why couldn't people just read a good book and get educated or entertained that way?

More annoyed than he should have been, he went back to the task at hand, sliding out his phone from his pocket.

A quick tap to open the camera, swipe to the record function, switch the camera view to selfie mode, and he was ready.

He'd taken photos on the tube before; many photos. But they'd been timid shots, snatched on the pretence of taking a selfie. None had been close enough of his targets. They hadn't revealed anything of them. He just hadn't been brave enough.

His online friends had not been impressed by his efforts.

But now they would be.

With a stretched, straight arm he held the phone as low as he could go, keeping it close to his body. He angled it until the camera was directed up towards the blonde girl, just below the line of her short skirt.

Pulse racing with excitement, he gazed down at the screen, hoping to see hidden delights, but was disappointed to see nothing.

It was too dark down there.

He moved the angle of the phone, but it was no use. Still, the screen remained black.

Damn.

He withdrew the phone and stopped the recording, feeling deflated and defeated.

But soon the anger overtook him again.

He would get what he was after.

He just needed to be patient.

~

He stayed close to her as the train rocked and bumped its way through the grime-ridden tunnels. Watching and waiting for her to disembark. This was when he would make his move.

The phone was still down by his side, his finger ready to bring it back to life.

And as the train slowed and came to a stop at Euston Square, his chance came.

The blonde girl hoisted her silver handbag onto her slender shoulder and exited the carriage. He followed, aiming to stay close, but a couple of middle aged tourists came in between them and thwarted his plan.

'It's okay, Jeremey, I have the directions here on this piece of paper,' the woman said, fishing about in her bag as she walked. 'The hotel is just a few minutes' walk away.'

She slowed, unable to produce it.

'C'mon, Margaret, you're blocking the way,' the man said, noticing the impatient, unsmiling young man directly behind them. He encouraged her forward with a gentle arm around her back. 'We can find it when we get out of here.'

He wanted to shove her hard. She was ruining everything. The blonde was getting away. And he needed to be right behind her. Unless he could get past these cretins, it would be over.

The escalators were just up ahead. He decided to be bold and squeezed past the two slow-goers with a shallow apology. A couple more deft manoeuvres through the exiting crowds and he was back behind her, just as they reached the escalators.

His hand was slick with sweat as he tried to swipe open the phone, and the device wouldn't recognise the touch.

Damn it!

Drying his hands on his trouser leg, now a quarter of the way towards the top, he tried again and the video function was activated.

Breathless from his panic, sweat dripping from his hair, he held the phone out in front of him, towards the girl on the step above and in front of him.

This time it was working perfectly.

He could see the white of her underwear and the cheeks of her bottom. He moved the phone that little bit closer to the girl, trying to get an even better video.

A video that would both impress his online friends and also give him pleasure.

Yes, that was even better!

Lost in the wonder of the images from the phone's screen, he didn't notice when they reached the top of the escalator, and he stumbled onto the walkway.

The phone slipped from his grasp and skidded across the floor like an ice hockey puck, narrowly avoiding being crushed underfoot by a number of people.

'Sorry, sorry,' he said, rushing for the device, which would still be recording. He snatched it up, with some relief, and shoved it back into his pocket.

'Hey, were you filming that girl?' someone said from behind him.

He turned to face the bearded, suited man, in his mid-fifties.

'No, of course not,' he managed. He forced a laugh. 'Don't be stupid.'

'I saw you,' he said, undeterred, as fellow travellers passed by them. 'This man, he was filming the girl, going up the escalator,' he directed at the passers-by. 'The phone, it was underneath her skirt.'

He had to get away.

'You're mistaken,' he said. 'I've got to go.'

He headed away from his accuser, head down. He had to get out of the station before someone stopped him.

'He was filming that girl!' the man said from behind him.

He kept going. The evidence was right there, on the phone. If there were police around, or station staff, they would catch him red handed.

He turned to see the businessman watching him, but not following.

Fortunately the barriers were just up ahead, and he felt a mixture of relief and elation as he passed through them unimpeded.

He emerged into the sunlight on the corner of Euston Road and Gower Street, putting some distance between him and the station, just in case the man had alerted the authorities.

He paused only when he got to Russell Square, and despite himself, couldn't help but watch the video and admire his creation.

The rush was just like before.

What a success!

His friends were going to be so impressed.

PART II

11

Cullen headed back to the tube, making his way through the ticket barriers and down deeper underground along the escalators. He exited left towards the westbound line, where he would head towards King's Cross. The platform was busy as usual, although the rush-hour crush had long gone, to be replaced by a mixture of tourists and daytime commuters. He glanced left and right on the platform, unable to switch off.

He always found it difficult to switch between civilian and police roles, but at the moment it was particularly hard, especially down in the tube network. Cullen was the lead officer for Operation Archangel, which was targeting sexual crime on the transport network in the capital. Involving hundreds of uniformed and plain clothes officers across the city's underground system, the operation had been running for several months and had already seen many arrests.

Just one week ago, on a tube carriage, Cullen had witnessed what he thought was a sexual assault. He had pursued the assailant, after being misled by the girl who Cullen had assumed had just been attacked. The chase had led to a dramatic and tragic conclusion, with a fatal road crash, a devastated girlfriend, and Cullen subject to the prospect of an independent police investigation. And although the investigation had been swiftly resolved in his favour, the event still troubled him.

The young man, Tyrone Green, who had been crushed beneath the wheels of a heavy lorry, wouldn't even have been buried yet.

Operation Archangel had been a tremendous success. Heralded by Chief Superintendent Maggie Ferguson, the operation had won plaudits among the London press for the way the transport police had taken on the scourge of the small yet dangerous minority of individuals who believed they could operate without fear underground. The operation was due to continue for the next three weeks, but such was the success that there had been calls to extend it indefinitely. The London Mayor in particular had been a vocal advocate for its continuing presence. But the truth was it would be hard to maintain the level of resources indefinitely. There just wasn't enough funding within the force to keep the intensity of the operation going on an ongoing basis.

Cullen had to hope that the short sharp shock of the operation would be enough to suppress the activities of those who might be tempted to offend on the network.

At least until the force could undertake a repeat operation the following year.

CULLEN EXITED the tube at Kings Cross station and made his way along the busy main street towards the Excelsior Hotel. The hotel was frequently used by the British Transport Police to put up visitors who had travelled from across the country to their headquarters in nearby Camden Town. The hotel offered a special rate, and for Cullen, the deal was even better. He could stay the night for just under fifty pounds, which was unheard of in central London, especially as the hotel was one of the better establishments.

He checked in at reception, then took the opportunity to freshen up and call Sarah from the room.

He updated her about Tony's condition, and let her know his plans for travelling back to Wigan early the next day. She was highly amused when she heard of the plans for that evening, and that Cullen was faced with having to watch his most hated musical.

'Well Paul, I must say, I'm really proud of you,' she said, the smile apparent in her voice.

'Yeah, I can't say I'm really looking forward to it,' he replied. 'But, I think it's the least I can do for the both of them, I'm just going to have to close my eyes and think of something else,' he said, deadly serious.

'Well I do think it's really nice of you,' she said. 'I'll be thinking of you tonight.'

'I'll survive,' he said, lying back on the bed and staring at the ceiling.

They talked some more about Philip. Sarah had already been to visit him, and her update about his condition was quite positive.

'He was quite bright today,' she said. 'Actually, he was the best I've seen him since I came back up here. Obviously it's all relative, but you really learn to take the small positives out of the situation.'

'I can imagine,' he replied. 'I'm really glad to hear that he was okay. When I get back tomorrow, I want to go and see him straight away. I've got an idea. Something that I hope will make a difference.'

'Sounds intriguing.'

Cullen nearly told Sarah there and then what he'd been afraid to tell her for so long, but he decided it would be much better to do it face-to-face, so he kept quiet and waited for another day.

12

Cullen decided to stretch his legs and walk the just under two miles to the British Transport Police Headquarters in Camden Town. Taking the backstreets, he covered the ground quickly and made the trip in just under twenty minutes.

He approached the headquarters, a high-rise office block on Camden Road, home to British Transport Police's Central Division, and the Major and Serious Organised Crime department that Cullen led. His team worked on serious cases across the country involving the rail network. While British Transport Police regional teams dealt with the less severe end of the criminal spectrum, Cullen's team were involved in the higher level crimes - murder, serious sexual assault, gang related activities, and other serious crimes. Their work took him across the country, in conjunction with the northern team, based in Leeds, which was headed up by DCI Harper.

Cullen had joined the team eight years ago, transferring

down from British Transport Police's Manchester division. He had climbed the ranks rapidly, from Sergeant to Inspector and now Chief Inspector, working under Chief Superintendent Maggie Ferguson.

Cullen entered the building and headed for the lifts, wanting to avoid Maggie Ferguson at all costs. She had told him to take a holiday, following his exploits the week before, where he had really pushed her loyalty with his informal investigation into Natalie Long's disappearance. And even though she had tipped him off about Tony's heart attack, he knew she wouldn't take kindly to seeing him back on the premises so soon, no matter what the circumstances.

'Boss,' surprised Detective Sergeant Alex Summers said as Cullen exited the lift. 'I thought you were on...'

DS Summers was a young, promising officer who had been with the team just under a year. Cullen had spotted the potential in him at interview, and he hadn't been disappointed by his performance since. He knew that this guy would have a bright future. He'd already been involved in numerous complex investigations, and had really made a difference in several with his quick instinct and sharp brain.

'Holiday,' Cullen finished the sentence. 'I am,' he said, 'but I just popped in for a few minutes while I was passing by, after seeing Tony.'

'Yes, of course,' he said. 'How is he? They told us about what happened at the team meeting this morning.'

'He's doing okay,' Cullen said, 'I'm sure he'll be back in action before we know it.'

DS Summers nodded. 'Tony is a strong guy. I just knew he'd pull through.'

Cullen said goodbye and headed to conference room one,

where the meeting about Operation Archangel was about to begin. He felt slightly guilty about gate-crashing the event, and knew that it might well put his deputy, Detective Inspector Danny Lomax on the back foot, but he was sure DI Lomax could handle it.

HE SLIPPED into the room via the back door, taking a seat in the corner, impressing himself by entering without being noticed. He was used to being the centre of attention at these kind of events, and was actually looking forward to just observing at the back for once.

DI Lomax, who also didn't seem to have noticed his boss entering, was talking to the room of invited guests, who had been lured to the event with the promise of a good lunch and an update on how the operation was going. Cullen scanned the room, spotting a number of familiar faces among the London stakeholders. Most of the people he recognised were from various parts of the London media. He could see Zack Carter, the young journalist from the London Daily Post, sitting off to the left. The guy, who he discovered last week came from the same part of the world as he did up in the north-west, had impressed him with his morals. Some of the visitors he recognised as being from the various charities in London associated with prevention of sexual crimes. They had a particularly good working relationship with these charities and it was one of the pleasures of the job to see the difference that they were making to those most vulnerable.

DI Lomax continued his presentation, his accent unmistakeably Essex, running through a series of slides that Cullen knew well. The slides outlined the main aims of Operation Archangel, the historical number of assaults reported on the tube network over the past few years, and the latest data on the number of arrests that had been made in the few months following the operation's existence. The audience appeared interested for the remainder of the presentation, and Cullen watched as Zack tapped away on his tablet.

Cullen hoped the headlines in the evening edition of the Post would be positive. You could never tell with that publication when the Deputy Editor, Simon Hardacre, was in charge. He was particularly ambitious and ruthless when it came to generating stories, and enjoyed provoking the force with dubious articles.

Trevor Goulding, the Editor, and a much more reasonable and principled man than his deputy, was currently on holiday.

'So,' DI Lomax said, as he reached the final slide. 'I'm going to open this up now to some questions. We've got a couple of microphones in the room, so if you have got a question could you please stick your hand up, and someone will be over with the mike so everyone can hear.'

A number of questions came forward, all quite reasonable and easy enough for DI Lomax to field. He was an experienced officer, having worked at British Transport Police for his whole decade-long police career. Transferring from the London regional team five years ago, he had quickly made himself a key member of the serious and organised crime department. And when Cullen had been promoted to DCI, he had had no hesitation in recommending the affable DI Lomax as his deputy.

Cullen watched as DI Lomax searched the room for any more questions. Despite his confidence, Cullen could see the tension turn to relief on his face as he didn't see any more hands.

'Well, if that's all the questions for today, we've just got lunch to come, so if you like...'

'Actually, I have got a question,' a voice said. 'It's about what happened last week, with your boss, DCI Cullen.'

13

Cullen tensed at the question. From his vantage point at the back of the room, it was unclear who was asking it. He strained his neck forward, to try and see who the questioner was. DI Lomax was directing his attention over towards the left hand side of the room, in the middle.

'I'm afraid I'm unable to comment about that specific incident,' DI Lomax replied, not missing a beat. 'I'm sure you will understand the need to protect those involved.'

Cullen was impressed by the way DI Lomax had dealt with a difficult question, and all without knowing that his boss was watching.

'Now, if we've all finished, I think we should take that break.'

'I think people deserve answers,' the questioner continued. 'The family and loved ones of Tyrone Green in particular, deserve more.'

DI Lomax turned back to look again at the man, and Cullen could see the frustration that his colleague was doing well to hide. There was always a risk with these kind of events, no matter how controlled the environment, that things might go awry.

But Cullen had confidence in his deputy, so remained impassive at the back, no matter how much he wanted to get involved.

'As I said, I think people need answers, especially when it might reveal failings of the current operation. A young man is dead, a young woman has been bereaved, I think it needs to be addressed.'

Now everyone from all across the room was tuned in to what the man was saying. He had the floor, and Cullen could see that DI Lomax was struggling to regain control.

Emboldened by the attention, the man continued, now standing up to emphasise his new-found position of authority.

Cullen struggled to remain in his seat.

'I appreciate what you said Detective, about the need to tackle the issue of sexual crime on the London transport network. Of course no one is going to argue that something needed to be done. For too many years our city and the people who should be there to look out for us, have turned a blind eye to these crimes and the victims.'

Cullen got his first proper view of the man, as he turned to address the back half of the room. He looked familiar, with his close-cropped balding head. But Cullen, usually very good with names and faces, couldn't quite put his finger on where he knew him from.

Thankfully his colleague came to his aid. 'And you are?' DI Lomax asked.

'Sorry, how rude of me. My name is Adrian Spencer, and I'm an investigative reporter for London Lines.'

Suddenly it became clear. A few months ago, Cullen had

seen this guy in a feature article in the London Daily Post, which had covered the story of the rise of the new online news site, London Lines. It hadn't been a complimentary article, and had been designed to torpedo the new challenger to their dominance of news coverage across the capital.

London Lines was one of the growing number of click bait funded news websites that trawled the Internet and beyond for stories that drew people in and powered advertising revenue. The article had explained how since its launch two years ago, the site had grown massively and was a phenomenal success. It was also a huge thorn in the side of both the mainstream media and the targets of its dubious journalistic practices.

As part of the story they had a focus on one of the lead reporters, Adrian Spencer, who had achieved a certain level of fame in recent years relating to the case of Emma Holden.

He had sold his story to a national newspaper, trying to capitalise on the distressing events involving the young actress and her friends. The move had backfired, when social media had turned on him for the role he had played in the situation, including impersonating a journalist at the London Daily Post.

But he had now reinvented himself and was once again causing trouble.

'I just wonder what you're going to say to the poor girl, Shazney Powell, who later this week will bury her boyfriend. A man killed in broad daylight as a result of overzealous policing. He died for no more reason than having a lovers' tiff.'

'As I said, we really can't talk about individual cases. It isn't appropriate.' DI Lomax was losing patience with the man, and Cullen was starting to get nervous. Not because he feared Adrian Spencer's questions, but because he feared how it would look if they didn't respond appropriately.

But once again he resisted the temptation to interject. Being a leader was as much about letting your team lead, and this was an ideal opportunity to put that into practice.

'I beg to differ,' Adrian Spencer insisted. 'I think it is *entirely* appropriate to talk about the matter in this forum. If not here, then where? We are here to discuss Operation Archangel, we are here to be able to ask questions, and maybe not just the easy ones you want us to ask.'

Suddenly a young man a few rows in front of Cullen noticed him. Cullen knew him as the communications lead at one of the women's charities he had liaised closely with over the past few months. The man seemed surprised by Cullen's presence, and then spoke to the person on his right, who also risked a glance.

Like some form of contagion, the news spread quickly and within just a few seconds, the commotion had attracted the attention of DI Lomax and Adrian Spencer.

Cullen felt he had no choice but to enter the fray.

~

As much as he had wanted to let DI Lomax take the lead, matters had got out of his control. Cullen strode down the middle aisle and made his way to the front, nodding at his colleague, who returned the gesture and took a symbolic step back to the side.

'Ladies and gentlemen,' Cullen began, eying the expectant audience. He took a particular lingering look at Adrian Spencer, who was still standing. Cullen took heart in the expression on Spencer's face; his bravado had disappeared in the face of Cullen's unexpected appearance. 'As many of you will know, last week there was a tragic incident at Euston, involving myself. As Mr Spencer here has already mentioned, a young gentleman very sadly lost his life.'

Cullen in the middle of his speech, had a split second flashback of the scene where Tyrone had been hit by the London bus, before being thrown under the wheels of the lorry.

'I very much regret the outcome of the incident, and the force and myself personally have been in touch with the man's family to say how sorry we are.' Again he pointedly looked at Adrian Spencer as he spoke the words. 'You may also have heard that the Independent Office for Police Conduct investigation decided unanimously that there were no grounds to take matters any further. I respect the decision of the OPC, and stand by my actions last week. However, that does not mean I take this young man's death lightly. As a police officer, my number one priority is and always has been to protect the people of this country. As such what happened last week does hurt. However, this should not detract from the magnificent effort that has been put in day after day by my officers during the current operation.'

Again he looked at Adrian Spencer. This time the man's face seemed to have regained some of its earlier bravado. Spencer consulted with a notebook in his hand.

'Last week's incident isn't the only one relating to your operation, DCI Cullen,' Adrian Spencer shot back. Again he looked down at the notebook. 'We've had a number of people contacting us to complain about heavy-handed police tactics. Innocent people going about their daily lives on the transport network, harassed by your officers, I'm afraid to say. One young boy who we spoke to has been left rather traumatised by an experience with one of your officers, who accused him of brushing up against a lady on the tube. This was despite the fact that the lady in question did not make any complaint and the young boy swears that any contact was just accidental.'

Cullen considered his response quickly but carefully. He was aware that anything he said might end up on the pages of London Lines, plus any other number of London media outlets currently present in the room. He needed to be extremely careful.

'If anyone feels they have been unfairly treated by any of my officers, then I would strongly encourage them to contact me personally and discuss the concerns.'

Adrian Spencer smiled, as if he had just got the response that he was hoping for. 'Does that invitation extend to Shazney Powell? I know she would like to speak with you. Are you prepared to face her and give her the answers that she so deserves?'

'Yes,' Cullen said without hesitation. He knew that this was not the answer his boss would've wanted him to give. Maggie Ferguson had been very clear about not engaging. But that had been before the conclusion of the investigation.

And what other choice did he have, being put on the spot like this?

Adrian Spencer nodded, satisfied and looking a little surprised by Cullen's response. 'She will want a third party at the meeting,' he said. 'Someone independent whom she trusts and can debrief with afterwards.'

'Of course,' Cullen replied.

'As you can imagine, she is still extremely upset and vulnerable, but she does want to do this, sooner rather than later.'

I bet she does, Cullen thought, under no illusions as to who this supposedly independent third person would be. But there was no way that he was going to meet Shazney with Adrian Spencer alongside. It just wasn't going to happen, although now wasn't the time to argue the point.

'We'll set it up,' Cullen promised.

Adrian Spencer was beaming as he sat down, like the cat that had got the cream.

Cullen turned to DI Lomax. 'Over to you,' he said. 'Nice to meet you all,' he said to the audience, before leaving the room and heading for the lift.

14

She lay back in the bath, thinking of him. He was intoxicating, all-consuming, and she longed to be with him again.

He'd only left the flat an hour ago, but it felt much longer.

She closed her eyes and remembered the events.

It had been amazing.

The best yet.

Good enough to dispel the guilt from what she had done.

What she was still doing.

To the one she loved.

She remained in the water until it went cold, and then nearly topped it up again. But she had things to do, work to get on with that she had put off in her euphoria.

Wrapped in a towelling robe, she padded into the living room and gazed out of the window across the city. A hand placed on the glass, she wondered where he was right now, and if he was thinking of her like she was thinking of him.

Once a cheater, always a cheater.

The voice of her grandmother warned her from beyond the grave.

But this was different.

It was meant to be.

Lost in her fantasies, she barely heard the phone ringing.

Panicking, not wanting to miss his call, she scrambled to find her mobile, down the side of the sofa, before it rang off.

But it wasn't him.

'Oh, hi,' she said, the guilt returning to her shore like a crashing wave. 'How's things?'

She listened to the response.

'Oh, that's good. It's great that you're feeling better...you are? Oh...are you sure? I mean, I thought you were set on the idea?...Well, if that's what you think's best, then I'm really happy for you. It will be fantastic to still have you around,' she managed to say.

After a few more minutes of conversation they ended the call.

She spun the phone across onto the sofa and paced around the room, stunned by the news. She felt like screaming, but the neighbours above and below would wonder what the hell was going on.

Instead she returned to the window, her head resting on the pane, her eyes closed and her mind whirring.

And then it came to her.

The perfect solution.

15

Cullen knocked and waited for the familiar voice of Chief Superintendent Maggie Ferguson to call out. He stepped into the room and closed the door softly behind him. Maggie Ferguson, a formidable police officer who had taken over at British Transport Police's Central Division after a successful career with Police Scotland, smiled and gestured for him to be seated.

'Well, Paul, I didn't expect to see you again here so soon,' she smiled, daring him for a response.

'Neither did I,' Cullen replied. 'This isn't exactly my idea of a holiday.'

'Yes,' she said playing with the biro on her desk, tapping it against the wood. 'You do seem to have an issue with actually taking leave.'

Cullen knew what she was referring to. His unofficial and unauthorised investigation the previous week had very nearly cost him his job, and had damaged the trust between him and Ferguson.

And that was the reason why he was here now.

'How was Tony?' she asked, softening.

'He's doing okay. He was a bit groggy, the drugs still hadn't worn off. But the operation seems to have been a success, and he was in pretty good spirits.'

'Well that's great news,' she said. 'It really is. I did fear the worst when the news first came through. Thank you for coming back down here, it reveals a lot about you as a person.'

'Tony is a good friend,' Cullen replied.

'So, are you planning to travel back up to the north-west, Wigan isn't it?'

'Tomorrow morning,' Cullen said.

'Good,' she nodded. 'I do think the break will do you good, after last week's excitement.'

'It was great to be with Sarah,' he agreed.

'How was the media briefing for Operation Archangel,' she asked.

Cullen was surprised that she knew he had been there.

'More eventful than I would've liked,' Cullen admitted, wondering whether someone had already tipped her off about what had happened.

'Oh?'

'A reporter from London Lines was there,' he explained. 'He challenged me about what happened last week with Tyrone Green, tried to use it to undermine the operation. And he's been in touch with the girlfriend, Shazney Powell. He wants me to meet with her.'

'No,' she said firmly. 'That would not be a good idea. I hope you told him as much?'

Cullen hesitated slightly.

Maggie Ferguson's face hardened. 'Please tell me you didn't agree to a meeting?'

'I didn't think I really had a choice,' he admitted. 'I was put on the spot.'

Maggie Ferguson shook her head ruefully. 'Bad idea,' she said. 'A *really* bad idea. Did anyone else hear you agree to this?'

'Just a room full of journalists.'

'Bloody hell, Paul,' she said, giving him a fierce glare. 'You do realise the comms team are going to go nuts when they find out about this? And there's no going back now, you're going to have to do it, we just need to find a way of making sure we keep control.'

'Indeed,' he said.

'Boss, I'm really sorry about what just happened,' DI Lomax said in his strongest Essex accent as Cullen entered the main investigation room. The large open plan office was relatively busy, with a number of his officers working at the computers. It was always a busy environment, dealing with investigations across the country. Several of his colleagues looked up and greeted him as they spotted their boss - evidently prepared for his appearance - and he smiled hellos at them before they dutifully moved back onto their work.

Cullen and Lomax moved into his office, and closed the door behind them.

'I presume the guy was not on the invite list?' Cullen could not conceive of any way in which they had deliberately invited a journalist from London Lines.

'No, he wasn't. I've just checked it now. He definitely wasn't on the list.'

'How did he get in then?'

DI Lomax looked pained. 'I checked with Lucy on the desk. He arrived at the last minute and talked his way in, saying that he worked for one of the charities. She didn't check his ID. She feels terrible about what happened.'

'I'll speak to her,' he replied. Lucy was a lovely lady, who had worked at the British Transport Police Headquarters for over five years. She would feel awful, he knew that. He would go down there in a few minutes to smooth things over. He would however be forced to address the issue with her, of how a person without due authorisation, could lie his way into the heart of headquarters and cause trouble.

He could imagine how Adrian Spencer would've been able to turn on the charm and lie his way through. But a simple check of his ID would have cut off his plans dead.

This had undoubtedly been a serious security breach, and should not have happened. Adrian Spencer had been an annoyance, but what if this had happened with somebody who had much more sinister intentions?

'So how's Tony?' DI Lomax enquired. The Chief Super told us the news this morning. We were all shocked.'

'He's doing okay, under the circumstances,' Cullen confirmed. 'But he'll need some time to rest.'

'You don't think this might be the trigger? To leave the stage?'

'Maybe,' he said. 'I know Brenda is hoping that's going to be the case - she wants to go on those around the world cruises. But you know Tony, I don't think it's going to be that straightforward.'

'No, I expect you're right.'

'Well done anyway for the way you dealt with Adrian Spencer,' Cullen said, changing the subject back to the incident upstairs. 'I thought you handled the guy well, and I wouldn't have interjected if the room hadn't spotted me at the back.'

'He took me by surprise, that's for sure,' he said reflecting on what happened. And it had been going so well.'

'Not to worry,' Cullen replied. 'I think the vast majority of people in that room know that what we're doing is for the good of all Londoners, and they could see through Adrian Spencer for the person that he is.'

'You're really going to meet the girlfriend?' Lomax said.

'I have to,' he said.

'You spoken to the Chief Super about it?'

'Just,' he revealed. 'As you can imagine, she is thrilled at the prospect of it.'

'I can imagine,' he laughed. 'Seriously though, Boss, it seems like an extremely risky move, don't you think?'

'Oh yes, it is risky. I'll just have to make sure I have my wits about me, and I'll be dammed if I'm giving Adrian Spencer and London Lines any ammunition.'

DI Lomax looked at him, thinking about something.

'What is it?' Cullen said, 'Spit it out.'

'Permission to be candid, Boss.

'Of course.'

'Something doesn't quite add up about all this,' he said. 'Yes, Adrian Spencer did put you on the spot up there, but you could easily have found a way of avoiding his request. I've seen you too many times, dealing with people like him. You didn't need to agree to meet the girl.'

Cullen couldn't help but smile. His colleague had zeroed in on something. His agreement to meet the girl was not totally driven by Adrian Spencer's public request.

'You want to meet her, don't you?' he smiled, his Hollywood-perfect white teeth almost shining. He clicked his fingers into a point at Cullen. 'Adrian Spencer gave you the cover to do it.'

Cullen nodded. 'Your powers of observation are impressive,' he jested.

'Why?' he said. 'Why do you want to meet her?'

'Because I think she deserves it,' he responded. 'She deserves to be able to ask her questions. I'm hoping it will help her, to deal with whatever she's going through.'

It was impossible to think of the case without reflecting on his own daughter, Amy, and how he would do anything for her, to soothe her pain. Just like he had done the week before.

And he would do the same for this girl.

'But will it help you?'

'Maybe,' he revealed.

'It's a risky strategy, Boss.'

'I know.'

'You know, Boss, there aren't many officers like you. Especially in the higher ranks.'

'Thank you, I think,' Cullen said.

'It was meant to be a compliment. But if I can be candid again.'

'Be my guest.'

'Just be careful, Boss. Don't let your good nature be the ruin of a great career. No one here will thank you for throwing yourself under a bus for your principles and your desire to help others. We need you here. And you know that you're giving Adrian Spencer and the lowlife London Lines just what they want.'

'Don't worry, I'm going to go into this with my eyes open, and I won't be giving that man what he craves.'

The bottom line was, he wanted to meet the girl, to listen to her side of the story, to try and help. If meeting with him would really help her cope with the loss of her boyfriend, in whatever circumstances it had happened, then he would do it. He would also do his upmost to extract her from the tentacles of London Lines and Adrian Spencer.

Despite all the risks.

16

He booted up the computer in the back bedroom and took a sip from his strong tea.

The home screen loaded, he clicked through to his folders and connected the phone via the USB cable.

Just a short time later, the video had been transferred onto the hard drive, catalogued with the same care and attention that he gave to all his output.

There were nearly a thousand photographs and videos taken by his own camera, and triple that taken by other people that he had harvested from the online communities he frequented.

He'd spent quite a deal of time considering how best to catalogue his treasure trove. After a couple of false starts, he'd gone with a hierarchical structure that started with broad age of girl (teen and below/young woman/older woman), then hair colour (blonde/brunette/redhead/other), then area of body (face/chest/legs/bottom/upskirt/other).

It allowed him to get to the right images and videos quickly.

Once the video was in place, he logged on to the portal.

It wasn't visible through search engines.

To the everyday browser it didn't exist.

Password entered, he was into the secure site and, as he always did, hungrily scanned the board for new uploads.

It was his thrice daily ritual.

His obsession.

There had been just a handful of uploads since his early morning check. That wasn't unexpected, as most of the active users were from the States, and would still be asleep.

Although a lot of users didn't seem to sleep much.

He checked out the new additions, for once wanting to be disappointed. He wanted to be the talk of the site today. He wanted his place at the top. He didn't want someone else coming along and usurping him.

But there was no worry. They were all photos, stills of women on the transit systems in North America - one he recognised as the Subway in New York, another San Francisco, while the third had been tagged Toronto.

They were standard photos - very pretty girls, of that there was no doubt - but nothing to really excite.

Or shock.

Now was his chance to shine.

~

HE CHECKED back on the site every few minutes over the next hour, each time frustration growing at the lack of response from the community.

He could see from the stats next to his upload *Blonde Upskirt* that people had clicked on it.

So why no comments?

Were they deliberately ignoring him and his creation?

Maybe they were jealous!

He smouldered around the flat for another hour, trying to distract himself with a game of Zombie Zone IV on the X Box, but unable to resist checking the site another half a dozen times.

Why did he even engage with this group of people?

And then the first comment came in. From a regular user.

Webslinger

Nice video, my man! Great shot of a great ass! One for the collection! Stay cool.

He sat there, beaming.

He had received acclaim from the one of the site's most respected users!

He tapped out a reply.

Cheers, my man!

He looked again at Webslinger's comment and his smile widened. It was praise indeed.

And yet he craved more. He stared at the screen, desperate for more response.

None came for the next, long thirty minutes.

And then the second comment.

Great video! Comedy gold.

He scrutinised the comment, unable to understand what the person, Turnpike, meant.

Comedy?

He waited for the user to elaborate, but no further response was forthcoming.

So he typed out a response.

Funny?

Turnpike came back almost immediately.

Yes, very funny!

He couldn't resist pressing him on this. How could he seek to undermine his video like this?

Why?!?

The ending is hilarious! ;)

Suddenly he realised what this was all about. He cursed himself under his breath. In his haste and excitement to share the video, he had completely forgotten to clip off the last part.

That guy nearly had you! You should be more careful in future! Run, rabbit, run! LOL!

He smacked the desk in anger at the ridicule. He hammered out an expletive-laden response, but thankfully decided not to press send.

Nothing from the site could be deleted.

Not comments.

Nor uploads.

Only the administrator could do that.

And that person had made it clear that this never happened.

So the unedited video showing him falling over, being challenged and running away, would be up for all to see.

Up there for all to laugh at.

How could he have been so stupid? He should have stopped to think. A few minutes, that's all it would have taken, to delete that final part.

He had ruined his opportunity.

And then he had an idea.

An idea how he could retrieve the situation.

He knew just what he had to do.

He would document the entire thing, from beginning to grisly end.

Then he would show *Turnpike* and all his other online friends what he was really capable of.

They would be so impressed.

He would be the hero of the entire community.

His name would be legend.

17

Cullen decided to pay a visit to Tony in hospital, before meeting Brenda outside the theatre, down by London's Strand. Tony had been in good spirits, more alert than in the morning, and had thanked him again for agreeing to accompany his wife to the performance.

The show itself wasn't exactly what Cullen would've called enjoyable. He hadn't suddenly miraculously been converted to the jazz-handed human cats prancing about the stage. In fact, sitting in the dark, the experience had been as painful as ever. However, he had consoled himself with the thought that he was doing a favour for a friend. And looking across at Brenda, lost in the wonder of it all, his spirits couldn't help but be lifted.

'Please tell me you haven't abandoned her like you did to me?' Sarah said, as a first response to Cullen's call through to her.

'It's the interval,' he protested. 'I've just come down to the bar to get a breather. Anyway, I did have stomach ache that night.'

'Okay, whatever you say,' she jested. 'I believe you, thousands wouldn't.'

'Alright, I admit it. The stomach ache wasn't that bad, but I did have a bit of discomfort. I swear.'

'Probably all that hot air,' she teased.

They continued the jovial chat for the next few minutes, before the bell sounded and it was time to go back.

'Good luck,' Sarah said.

'Thank you, much appreciated.'

'Seriously though, Paul, I'm proud of you for putting yourself through this personal hell.'

Cullen returned to the auditorium and took his seat next to Brenda, who was just finishing off an ice cream tub.

'Did you want one?' she asked. 'I was going to get you one, but I didn't know which flavour.'

'It's fine,' Cullen waved away. 'I'd rather just focus on the show,' he added mischievously. The lights dimmed and Cullen braced himself for another period of pain. His only solace was that he knew the second part of these shows was always shorter than the first.

AFTER THE SHOW Cullen accompanied Brenda back to her house in East London. Tony and Brenda lived in West Ham, once a working class area of the city, but now like everywhere in London, increasingly gentrified as the wealthier but not wealthy enough sought out new places and spaces to live that were within their budget. Tony was a massive West Ham United fan, and still spoke with sorrow at his club's move away from the old Upton Park ground to the massive Olympic Stadium in nearby regenerated Stratford.

Brenda repeated her earlier offer for him to stay the night, and it was tempting at that late hour to accept and crash out in the guestroom. She even showed him the room, the double bed made up ready for him, the space cosy and welcoming. He very nearly accepted. But his bag was back at the hotel, and it would be so much more convenient in the morning to travel to Euston from there.

'Thank you, Paul, I had a lovely evening, and I really appreciate you taking the trouble to accompany me tonight. I just wouldn't have wanted to go on my own, not with Tony how he is.'

'It was my pleasure. Happy birthday, Brenda.' Cullen gave her a friendly kiss goodbye on the cheek before heading back to the tube.

CULLEN SETTLED down in the tube carriage as the train rocked its way towards its destination. During the journey, Cullen, to his annoyance, couldn't help but reflect on the critical words of Adrian Spencer.

Had they been too draconian during Operation Archangel?

No matter what the circumstances, he had jumped to the wrong conclusion a week earlier when he had seen the two people across the carriage from him. He had been sensitised to any signs of sexual misdemeanours underground, and it had led to that man's death.

But as the train continued its journey, he rejected and shook off Adrian Spencer's accusations. His officers had been well prepared for the operation and he had every confidence in them. The task that they had been given was difficult. The London underground system saw approximately two million users a day, crammed into tightly packed metal tubes and ageing station passageways. It was an incredibly difficult environment to detect and apprehend criminal activity. But they had been very successful. And for that he was suitably proud.

Adrian Spencer was playing a very specific game, and Cullen was determined that he was not going to hand him anything that he wanted.

He would also put a stop to their influence on Shazney Powell.

He felt sure that they were taking advantage of the girl's grief and anger. It wasn't right. But it wasn't surprising either. Cullen knew many good journalists, professionals who were dedicated to reporting in a fair and truthful manner, without resorting to manipulation. But unfortunately he also knew a number who would go to seemingly any lengths to get a story, to make money, to further their career.

The trick was to identify the good from the bad.

Zack Carter from the London Daily Post was one of the good ones. He had only met him the one time the previous week, but Cullen had a strong instinct for good character, and that single meeting had convinced him.

In the coming days he would call him, and discuss the plans he had formulated for the meeting with Shazney.

He would infuriate Adrian Spencer, and that only made things all the sweeter.

18

Despite the anticipation of that evening's date with Ruben, the day passed quickly, as Olivia threw herself into her work. Three meetings later and the day was over. She had managed to refrain from telling the office about her meet-up with Ruben. She felt self-conscious and didn't want to set herself up for a fall, should the night not turn out as planned.

The Dog and Duck was a short fifteen minute walk from her flat. Ruben had said that the open mike was starting at half past seven, and he was one of the first on the bill, so they decided to meet just before half past and get in a quick drink before the performance.

Ruben was waiting for her as she entered the pub, which was already filling up with people.

Ruben stood as she approached. 'Great to see you,' he smiled widely. Olivia took a seat as Ruben asked for her order and went to get the drinks from the bar. Olivia looked across at the stage to her right, which was already set up with a single high stool and microphone on a stand. She imagined Ruben playing his guitar, making eye contact as he sang.

'Here you go,' Ruben said as he slid back into the seat after placing the two pints on the table. 'So,' he said, 'please be gentle on me when I take to the stage.'

Olivia smiled. 'Somehow I don't think I'll have to soften any blows,' she replied. 'I can imagine you're pretty good.'

Ruben took a sip from his Guinness. 'What makes you think that?' he asked, from over the glass.

'I just get the feeling that you're pretty good at everything you do,' she said.

If Ruben had been embarrassed by the flattery, he didn't show it.

'Everyone has their weaknesses,' he said in all seriousness, before taking another sip from the Guinness as he looked over at the stage.

'What do you play?'

'Lots of different things,' he said. 'Classic rock, folk, you know, anything that involves the guitar.'

'You've been playing since you were young?'

'Started at eight,' he replied. ' Learnt it at school. We had a really good teacher - he was pretty inspirational.'

'I used to play violin,' Olivia revealed. 'I was actually pretty good, was in the local orchestra, but I haven't played for a few years now.'

'You should start playing again,' Ruben said. He looked at her. 'I mean it, I can see the look of regret on your face, it would do you the world of good to get playing again, believe me. There's not much worse in life than a talent wasted,' he added with another sip of his drink.

Olivia thought on that statement. She didn't really think of herself as talented regarding the violin playing, but maybe she had been guilty of underestimating herself. 'Maybe I will,' she said at last.

'You definitely should,' he said. 'I'll be disappointed if you don't.'

Olivia didn't have chance to reply, as suddenly over the pub's soundsystem a voice introduced the beginning of the open mike session, and announced Ruben as the first performer.

Ruben took one last gulp of his drink, before smiling at Olivia and grabbing the guitar which had been propped up against his chair.

Ruben took to the stage like a professional, perching on the high stool and thanking the pub audience for their applause which had surprisingly erupted as he had taken to the stage.

Olivia looked around at all the people who were now focused on Ruben.

A thought came to her.

Have they all come to see him?

There was certainly a lot of people in the pub, and most of them were focused on Ruben.

'Good evening everybody,' Ruben began. He looked over at Olivia and said, 'I'd like to dedicate this evening's set to a really special friend. She knows who she is.'

And with that Ruben began playing. He was amazing. He was without doubt a very talented guitarist, running through a number of classic songs with ease. But his voice too was impressive. In fact throughout the mini set he had the crowd in rapture. Every song was finished with an enthusiastic round of applause, whistling and even some whooping. It really did resemble a mini concert, and one that the audience had been willing members. It certainly didn't seem like a simple open mike slot.

Ruben ended with the classic U2 song With Or Without

You. His voice soared and dipped with emotion that really drew you in, and when Ruben looked over at Olivia as he delivered the final few lines she felt herself welling up.

The song and set ended, and the whole pub, Olivia included, erupted in cheers.

'Thank you, thank you so much,' Ruben smiled as the applause died down. 'If you enjoyed tonight's set, or even if you didn't, just a quick reminder that you can donate to the charity appeal on my Just Giving page. One hundred percent of the money will go towards the restoration of schools in Northern Nepal, following the recent earthquake. You've all already been so generous since I started performing here, and it's made a huge difference. You can go on my website and find details of how your money is already helping the community. Thank you so much, and see you next week hopefully.'

And with that Ruben returned to a stunned Olivia.

'So,' he said, a sheen of sweat on his brow, 'did you enjoy it?'

'It was amazing,' Olivia replied. 'Honestly, it was one of the best live sets I've ever seen.'

'Thank you. You're very kind.'

'I'm not being kind, I'm just being honest.' Olivia looked around, 'I mean, look at the way that everyone reacted in here - they love you.'

Ruben shrugged. 'I just try my best.'

'Well honestly it was just amazing,' Olivia said. She looked around again at the pub. Everyone had gone back to the conversations and drinking. Up on the stage a guy was preparing for the next artist. 'So you've been doing this for a while?'

'Quite a few weeks now,' Ruben replied. 'I wasn't really planning to, but one of my friends convinced me and it went pretty well. It was just going to be a one off, but then the landlord asked if I'd come back the next week and I had the idea of raising some money through it. Since then it's taken off and I've got a regular gig.'

'I think that's really lovely,' Olivia said, 'raising money for the school in Nepal.'

Ruben nodded. 'I've been out there, volunteering. It's such an amazing place, the people are just the best, but they don't have much and with the way the climate is going it's just getting harder and harder for them. So anything I can do to help, I will do.'

'Like I say, it's a really lovely thing. How much have you raised?'

'Just under £2000,' he revealed. 'People have been really generous.'

'Wow,' Olivia remarked. 'I'm so impressed.' For the first time since she had met Ruben, he looked embarrassed by the flattery. It just made him even more attractive.

'Were you ever in a band?' Olivia asked.

'No,' Ruben said quickly. He took a long series of glugs from his drink, his eyes peering above the glass but focused on the wall behind her.

Ruben brought down the drink and they sat in silence for a few seconds. Olivia wondered what she'd said that was so wrong.

'What made you ask that?' Ruben said at last.

'I just thought that you might have been in a band, back

in New Zealand,' Olivia said, feeling strangely defensive for asking what she thought had been a perfectly reasonable question. 'I mean, you look so natural, sitting up there, I can imagine you being the lead singer.'

Ruben nodded, as if he had been convinced by her explanation in a way that she didn't really understand. 'Back in college a few of us did get together to play for a while, but it wasn't anything serious.' He finished the remnants of his drink. 'Would you like another?' he asked, raising the empty pint glass.

Olivia asked for the same again, and watched as Ruben moved across to the bar. As she was watching she saw a girl approach him. As Ruben and the girl chatted at the bar, Olivia was disappointed in herself to find that she was jealous of this innocuous encounter.

She distracted herself with her phone, scrawling through her Instagram feed. It was so effective that she failed to notice Ruben returning.

'Hey, Olivia, I'd like to introduce you to a friend of mine.'

Olivia looked up at the girl from the bar. With her sun kissed skin and blonde hair, wearing a casual t-shirt, she reminded Olivia of a surfer chick.

'Hi,' the girl smiled, taking Olivia in. 'Stephanie,' she said, holding out a hand. 'Pleased to meet you.'

'Olivia,' she said, taking her hand.

'It's really lovely to meet you, Olivia,' she said. 'Sorry, I can't stop, got to meet a friend in town.' Stephanie glanced at Ruben. 'Hope you both have a lovely night.'

'Stephanie was the person who persuaded me to perform here,' Ruben revealed, as they both watched the girl exit the pub. 'So I owe her one.'

'Is she also from New Zealand?'

Ruben nodded. 'We met here though. I didn't know her back home. I mean, there are more sheep than people in New Zealand, but we don't all know one another.'

That comment got a laugh.

They spent the rest of the evening in deep conversation, before Ruben accompanied Olivia home. At the doorstep there was a minute or so of nervous conversation before a goodnight peck on the cheek turned into more. And before Olivia knew it, they were inside her flat, kissing passionately and pulling off clothes, hungry for one another.

Later, Olivia lay next to a sleeping Ruben, watching his chest rise and fall with each breath, giddy with the thrill of what had just happened.

It wasn't weird was it, to just stare and admire?

She placed a hand on his head and enjoyed the feel of his thick, dark hair. Sliding close to him she cupped her body behind his and was soon drifting into sleep.

But just as her body was succumbing, a buzz from a phone by the bed called her back.

Ever so slightly disorientated, she reached across Ruben to grab the phone, and read the message on the home screen before realising it wasn't her device.

It was from Stephanie, the girl from the bar.

Bet you didn't expect to hear from me again?

And then as Olivia was still considering this in the semi-darkness, a second message came through.

Leave her alone. Or I'll tell her everything.

Self-conscious at the accidental invasion of privacy, Olivia quickly slid the phone back onto the drawers next to the bed, being careful not to disturb the still-sleeping Ruben. She shifted away from him ever-so-slightly, laying on her back, staring at the ceiling, prickles of nervous sweat forming on her skin.

What the hell was it all about?

PART III

19

Cullen had just stepped onto the platform at Angel tube station when he heard the announcement over the tannoy. The southbound line had been suspended due to a customer incident. He moved swiftly past the other disembarking passengers and turned through the archway towards the southbound platform.

Two London Underground workers were walking purposefully in the same direction, their faces serious, and Cullen caught up with them.

'Detective Chief Inspector Paul Cullen, British Transport Police,' he said bringing out his ID as they continued their walk. 'What's happened?'

One of the workers glanced at Cullen's ID card before replying. Neither of them slowed their pace.

'Someone has fallen onto the tracks,' the older of the two men explained. 'The alert just came through. It's only just happened.'

Cullen followed them through the archway to the platform. There was quite a significant crowd of people there, milling around with a distinct chatter that went with these situations.

Some people were visibly upset.

Two other London Underground workers were cajoling the people towards the escalators, but they were only having limited success at moving them.

Cullen and the two workers moved through the people, and through the entrance to the southbound platform. Here the crowds had been dispersed, and the platform was clear, save for the group of London Underground staff grouped together up ahead.

As they closed in, Cullen could see that the paramedics hadn't yet arrived. All London Underground workers were trained in first aid, just like the police, and at least two staff members in each station were trained in enhanced first responder skills. But they would only be able to do so much for someone who had fallen onto the tracks.

It would be a matter of doing the best they could until the paramedics arrived. And that could be anything from a few minutes to possibly ten or fifteen, depending on their availability and how quickly they could get down to the platform with all their kit.

The three of them reached the group tending to the person who had fallen. Just a matter of metres from them stood the now evacuated tube train that had somehow managed to stop in time.

'The track is safe,' the lady said as they arrived. 'Power is off.'

'I should think so,' one of the men who had accompanied Cullen replied, as they looked down at the three workers on the line. Cullen guessed that this man was the station manager.

'What happened?' the man asked the lady. 'The message was that she had fallen.'

The lady nodded. 'There were a number of witnesses.'

'So we don't think she was a jumper?' the man followed up.

'I don't think so. According to the witnesses she seemed to trip or stumble off the platform.'

'There was no alert in that regard,' he said, 'so if she did jump, then it's unlikely that she'd been planning it at the station in advance.'

Cullen knew what he was referring to. Recently the tube network had introduced a sophisticated monitoring system that utilised the thousands of cameras across the network, combining this with artificial intelligence technology to flag any concerning behaviour by passengers. It had already proved invaluable a number of times in identifying people who were considering taking their own life down in the depths of the London underground. It would spot patterns of behaviour, repeated trips to stations without boarding trains, lingering on platforms, standing too close to the edge as trains approached.

As part of Operation Archangel, Cullen had been in discussions with senior figures on the network as to whether such artificial intelligence could be directed to detect sexual offenders. And although it was early days, there was potential for this. It could be a game changer.

Cullen gazed down at the stricken figure of the woman.

'How is she?' he asked.

The lady hesitated as she seemed to only just realise that someone she didn't recognise was standing in front of her.

'Sorry,' Cullen said, 'I'm Detective Chief Inspector Paul Cullen, British Transport Police.'

'Wow, you were quick,' she replied, impressed at the speed at which he had materialised at the scene.

'I just happened to be getting off a northbound train,' he revealed. 'I mean we're good, but we're not that good.'

'I see,' she said. 'Well, the guys down there are doing their best, but she's got a pretty nasty head injury from the fall. We are just holding on until the paramedics arrive. We've heard that they're almost here, thank the Lord.'

'Just how bad do you think she is?' the senior worker asked.

'She is conscious, but we're not getting much sense out of her. Fortunately she didn't fall across the live rail and the train managed to stop in time. Otherwise there would have been nothing anyone could do.'

Cullen had seen the after effects of a person falling onto live rails. It was a gross under-exaggeration to say that it was not a pleasant sight. One of the most traumatic cases over the past few years was of a teenage girl who had been electrocuted after falling onto the tracks, under the influence after a night out with friends.

Feeling helpless watching the situation unfold below him, Cullen was relieved to see the paramedics arrive and quickly take control of the situation. The underground workers retreated back onto the platform and gathered alongside Cullen and the others.

'Are the police on the way?' Cullen asked.

'They've been called,' the man replied.

It would be the London division who would respond. The regional guys dealt with most first responder issues across the city, ranging from the more minor offences such as trespassing, to the most major of crimes, including suspected murder.

It was only after that initial assessment that Cullen's team, the Serious and Organised Crime unit, would be called in where appropriate. Cullen had a good working relationship with the London team, and their paths crossed often. The vast majority of serious offences on the railway network occurred in the capital, so whereas in the rest of the country the regional teams dealt with the vast majority of crimes on the railway, in London the split was much more balanced, with frequent handovers and sometimes joint investigations between the two.

~

UNIFORMED BRITISH TRANSPORT POLICE arrived a few minutes after the paramedics. He knew the two officers. One of them, Police Constable Caitlyn Newlove, had undertaken a secondment with Cullen's team the previous year and had impressed him with her intelligence and sharp instincts. The other, Gary Weston, was an experienced sergeant who had patrolled the London transport network for more than two decades.

Cullen and Gary had worked together on numerous cases over the past few years.

Cullen briefed the two on what he knew of the incident and all three of them retreated from the paramedics, who were still tending to the young woman on the tracks.

'Do we have any ID yet?' Gary enquired.

'Not yet,' Cullen replied, having asked the same question of the underground workers just a few minutes ago. He had noticed a bag lying next to the girl, but as yet no one had disturbed it. And it hasn't seemed a priority at that particular moment. But they would need to know very soon. Hundreds of people had been in the vicinity of the incident, with some seeing it directly. There would be no doubt that this was already out on social media. And soon it may well hit the mainstream media too.

They would need to find and contact the family before they found out via these other sources.

And right on cue, the Station Manager approached holding up a purse.

'Just been handed to me. I haven't looked inside.' He passed the purse to Cullen, who immediately clicked open the item. Inside was a selection of bank cards, with the name Dr Emily Roberts. And tucked inside one of the compartments, the girl's driving license, giving her address in Islington, North London.

'She's an academic at the London School of Global Health,' Cullen said as he examined another of the cards. It was the University ID card. 'Works in the Department of Infectious Diseases.'

'Home address?' Gary asked.

Cullen passed him the driver's license.

'I'll get one of the team over there now,' Gary said, looking at the address.

'Thanks,' Cullen replied. He handed the purse over to Caitlyn. 'You better keep hold of this. After all, this is going to be your investigation.'

'On that note,' Gary said, 'we'd better make a start on those witness statements. How many are there?'

'Six who put their hands up as being near Emily when she fell,' Cullen confirmed. 'The station manager has got them waiting in the office upstairs.'

'Great,' Caitlin said, with her trademark enthusiasm that he remembered well from her time at headquarters. 'Let's get cracking.'

'Paul, great to see you,' Gary said. 'Let's catch up with a pint sometime soon.'

'Definitely,' Cullen replied.

He said his goodbye but as he watched them walk away, something made him think, and he jogged to catch them up.

'Mind if I tag along?' he asked.

'Not at all,' Gary said with a smile. 'We can take two witnesses each if you like. Share the load around. If you've got nowhere better to go,' he added cheekily.

'Actually, I haven't,' he said.

20

The six witnesses were waiting nervously in the station control room, which was located back up the escalator and towards the exit. The control room was where the Station Manager and his small team monitored all activities, including those of both trains and passengers.

Cullen smiled and nodded at the waiting passengers, who just half an hour ago would never have imagined that they would be now participating in a police investigation. Of the six witnesses, four were men. The two suited younger men looked like late night commuters, possibly having worked late at the office, or maybe en route from some afterwork drinks. The other two men he wasn't so sure - one was a bearded gentleman of around sixty, and the other could've been no more than a late teenager. The two ladies were evidently friends, as they chatted quietly between themselves, both seemingly in their mid-thirties.

As Gary had suggested, they took two witnesses each, and fortunately there were two breakout rooms. Both were no larger or more salubrious than a broom cupboard, but they had chairs and offered privacy for the conversations. Caitlyn took one room, and Cullen the other, while Gary interviewed his two in the main control room.

The group were asked to wait outside while Gary, Caitlyn and Cullen asked them in one at a time. First Cullen interviewed one of the suited men. His name was Tom Thornbury. A worker in a major accountancy firm, he had been on his way home after an evening meal with work colleagues.

'I'm afraid I didn't see very much,' he admitted. 'I wasn't really looking around. But I did notice the lady brush past me, just before the train entered the station. I thought it was a bit strange, how she did that, because the platform wasn't that busy at the top end where we were. I'm used to a little bit of barging during the rush hour, you know when people struggle to get onto the train, but it seemed a bit unusual that she made contact when there was space just down from me.'

'Go on,' Cullen prompted.

'Well you know, before I could actually understand what was happening she just seemed to disappear off the platform. And then I heard a scream coming from my right I think, another passenger, screaming, something like "she's on the track". And the noise of the train, the screeching of the brakes it was so deafening, I just don't know how it managed to stop in time. I just remember thinking, that it was some kind of miracle that the train didn't hit her.'

'And as far as you can tell, she jumped?'

'Well, you know, I think so.'

'How confident are you?'

'Well, you know, I think, I would say that as far as I could see, she did jump onto the track but I can't be certain of course, so maybe eighty percent certain?'

The man looked up at Cullen as if he was answering some

kind of quiz question and was seeking assurance that his answer had been correct. Of course this was not a quiz. But it was a test. It was a way of testing the witness's certainty and confidence in their own account. It was a tried and tested method, to get the witness to question themselves and offer self-challenge.

Cullen nodded. 'So what could the other twenty percent be?' Cullen probed.

The man looked puzzled at first, but quickly began to think. 'Well, I guess if she didn't jump then maybe she just fell. Maybe, she was caught off balance, maybe she'd been drinking?'

'Is there anything that leads you to believe she had been drinking?'

'No,' he replied. 'I didn't smell any alcohol, but then, I wasn't really next to her for long enough, I wouldn't really have noticed even if she had been drinking. As I say, it all happened so fast, I just didn't really have time to take it in before it had already happened, if you understand what I mean.'

'I do,' Cullen replied. 'Is there any other explanation you can think of as to why she might have ended up on the tracks?'

The man thought for a moment. 'No,' he said finally. ' I can't think of anything else. I just hope that she's okay.'

~

THE SECOND INTERVIEWEE, one of the two lady friends, backed up the man's account. She also noticed the lady push past towards the edge of the platform as the train approached. But unlike the man, she was more minded to believe that it had just been a tragic accident. It was interesting how these two people, who had been standing no more than a couple of feet away from one another, and that witness the same action, could come to quite different conclusions.

Cullen saw this kind of thing all of the time. It was quite a generalisation, but he had noticed over the years that there was a distinct gender difference when it came to the interpretation of events. He was in no way a psychologist, but he had learnt over time that the person witnessing any event did so often through a lens that was made up of their own beliefs and experiences.

'Yes, I would say that I am ninety percent certain that she did just fall. She seemed to be in a hurry, so that would make sense wouldn't it?'

'There is every possibility,' Cullen replied. And there was, each year on the network dozens of passengers fell onto the tracks. For many alcohol played a part, but for others it was just simply a stumble.

'Do you think she might have meant to do that? 'The lady suddenly asked, her face darkening at the thought. 'Do you think she wanted to take her own life?' She looked disturbed by that prospect.

'I really don't know,' Cullen replied, 'but we'll do our very best to find out.'

'Oh, I really do hope that it was just an accident. I wouldn't want to think that she had intended for it to happen.'

Cullen finished the interview and waited until all six were completed, before reconvening with Gary and Caitlyn in the main room of the control centre. Up above them on the wall was a bank of television screens, relaying live footage from across the station. Cullen noticed that the screen on the far right was showing the southbound platform. The train was still there and he could see the group of workers at the far end.

The three of them exchanged notes from their interviews. All six witnesses had been consistent in their descriptions of the event. Four of those questioned had mentioned that the girl had brushed past people to get to the edge of the platform. Opinion was split as to what had led to her falling onto the track. A majority of four, all of the men, believed that she had jumped. One of the men thought the girl had looked scared or panicky. The two female friends meanwhile felt that she had fallen, although all three officers wondered whether this was because they had had chance to consult one another before being interviewed.

'A split decision then,' Gary said as they finished the debrief.

'Looks like we'll be going to the video referee,' Cullen said.

'The camera never lies,' Gary quipped.

'But it often doesn't tell the full story,' Caitlyn added.

'Quite right,' Cullen agreed. The thousands of cameras across the tube network were a godsend. And hundreds of cases had been solved at least partly through the revelations that they provided. But they didn't always have the answers. For one, there wasn't one hundred percent coverage across the network. And also, the picture quality, while vastly improved over recent years, wasn't always good enough.

'We can go through the images,' Gary said.

'Yes, let's get it done.' Cullen was looking at the screen again on the far right, he could see the group of workers walking back down the platform.

'Hopefully we'll get to ask Emily herself,' Gary added.

'Hopefully,' Cullen echoed. Something about the way the group were walking back down the platform, heads down towards the ground, set him on alert.

And then the Station Manager returned. All three officers knew what his expression meant.

'I'm afraid it's bad news,' he said.

21

The three of them were leaving the station when the Station Manager called them back.

'Scuse me officers,' he said. 'We've got another witness.'

The police officers turned as one.

'They've come forward following the initial media reports. Said they recognised the photo of the lady.'

The speed at which investigations progressed in the age of social and Internet media still impressed Cullen. It wasn't that long ago that the printed press was the quickest method of getting new leads, and it was always a struggle to get coverage, especially the stories that had fallen out of favour. But nowadays the photographs of those involved in police investigations were out almost immediately, and exposed to a level of scrutiny that had never been possible before.

'I just got a call down now from the entrance. Would you like me to send the witness down here?'

'Would you like to take this one, Paul?' Gary asked. 'If you and Caitlyn take this, I'll try again to make contact with the next of kin. Now that the news is out there, I'm afraid that someone is going to get a terrible surprise if we don't act quickly.'

They had tried to make contact with any family just after finding out the identity of the woman. But her belongings didn't have any clues or contacts numbers, and her employer was closed. Her phone was currently locked, and it would take time to be able to access it.

'Of course,' Cullen said, rather pleased that he had been allowed to take the lead on this additional interview. He was intrigued at what this new witness had to say, and whether they could shed any more light on what had happened. 'As long as Caitlyn doesn't mind her new partner,' he added with a smile.

'Not at all,' Caitlyn replied, in on the joke.

Gary played along. 'Well, I guess it's better to have loved and lost, than to have never loved before. Do treat her well, won't you?'

CULLEN AND CAITLYN accompanied the Station Manager back to the office. A couple of minutes afterwards, there was a knock at the door and one of the tube workers led in the new witness. She was a girl around her late twenties, Cullen estimated. She looked nervous, and completely out of place in her summery skirt and jacket.

Cullen stood up to greet her, wanting to put her at ease. He knew that being interviewed by the police was often an intimidating experience, no matter how much they tried to put people at ease. 'Detective Paul Cullen,' he smiled, proffering a hand. 'British Transport Police. And this is my colleague, Police Constable Caitlyn Newlove.'

Caitlyn also shook her hand. 'Pleased to meet you.'

They all sat down in the main room, as the Station Manager and his assistant left them to it. The three of them took their seats.

'So,' Cullen began. 'You think that you might have some important information regarding this evening's incident?'

'I think I might,' she said, her accent Australian. 'I mean, I saw the photo, of the lady, it was on Twitter, and I'm pretty sure that I saw her just before it happened.'

'If I could just take your details,' Cullen said, as Caitlyn stood by with her notebook.

'Oh, yes, of course,' the girl replied. 'Yes, my name is Bronwen. Bronwen Taylor. I work just down the road, at the Intercontinental Hotel. I'm the Restaurant Manager.'

Caitlyn took down the details.

'So, Bronwen,' Cullen continued, 'Tell me what happened.'

'Well, it was as I was just about to get onto the escalator, near the entrance of the station. I saw a lady, I think, well, you know I'm pretty sure that it was the lady who was on the track, and she seemed to be scared.'

Cullen glanced across at Caitlin, who he could tell was thinking what he was thinking. It was that reference to her being scared again. The picture was forming, and it could take this investigation in a very different direction.

'What makes you think she was scared?' Cullen probed.

'Well, it was the look on her face. I could just see, that she looked frightened, it really made me notice her. She was standing just in front of me on the escalator, and she kept looking back over her shoulder. You know, that sort of thing isn't really normal on the tube, is it? Normally people just have their head down. But she was really looking back, and I thought, that she was looking for someone in particular. And the look on her face, I remember thinking, it wasn't someone that she wanted to see. It was someone that she was scared of.'

'And then what happened?' Cullen asked.

'Well, we reached the bottom of the escalator, and I must admit, I did actually watch her as she walked towards the other platform. I was trying to see if I could spot someone who might have been following her. I did a quick look around, but there wasn't anyone obvious. So, I left it at that, didn't really think anything of it. I kind of convinced myself that there was nothing untoward, and maybe she was just in a hurry, or stressed about something.'

'So you definitely didn't see anyone who you thought might have been following her?' Caitlyn asked. 'No one at all?'

'No,' she confirmed. 'I didn't see anyone that looked to be following her. But, now I know what happened, I am thinking that maybe there was more to it.'

'Thank you for coming to speak to us,' Cullen said. 'We really appreciate it.'

The girl looked troubled. 'You know, when the commotion happened, no one knew what was going on. I didn't think for one minute that it involved her. We were moved out quite quickly, there was a bit of panic, people not knowing what was happening. But outside the station, when I checked social media, that's when I saw her picture. And I thought, that was the girl, the person who I'd been concerned about, and now look what had happened. It made me feel sick to my stomach. You know, that maybe I could've done something, something that would've prevented what happened from happening.'

'I really don't think you could have been expected to have prevented what happened,' Cullen replied. 'What you're doing now, this is a real help, so thank you. But please, don't be hard on yourself. Hindsight is a wonderful thing.'

The girl nodded, but didn't seem sufficiently soothed by his words. She looked up at Cullen. 'Is she okay? Is the girl going to be okay?'

Cullen shook his head sadly, watching the pained expression on his interviewee as realisation hit. The girl cupped her hands to her face, her eyes wide and watery.

Caitlyn reached over and placed a hand on her shoulder.

Cullen looked on. If this girl in front of him was right in her suspicions, then this potentially sexually motivated crime would be his investigation to take forward.

And he couldn't wait to get stuck in.

Already he was planning his next steps.

22

Olivia woke to an empty bed. She glanced at the table side clock radio, confirming that she'd overslept her usual wake-up time by an hour.

It was just before seven am.

After reading the mysterious text messages, she had taken some time to fall asleep. Olivia had had a sudden urge to rewind the evening, questioning what the hell she was doing - sharing a bed in her flat with a guy who she didn't really know anything about. But of course turning back time wasn't an option, so she had no choice but to sleep on it and regroup with her thoughts in the cold light of the morning.

And here she was.

But no Ruben.

Maybe it had all been in her imagination, like the ending of a child's story. Maybe the whole thing, the invitation, the open mike, the aftermath, had been just an incredibly vivid dream.

Or maybe Ruben was in the shower.

She made her way across the room and out into the small

hallway, listening out for any signs of activity. But the kitchen was empty, and there was no noise coming from the bathroom.

Given the time, and the fact that Ruben would probably have wanted to go home and get changed before travelling into work, he'd more than likely shot off.

Maybe he'd left a text message.

Her phone was still in her jeans pocket, left strewn at the bottom of the bed during their moment of passion.

But there was no message.

Ruben had just upped and left, without bothering to say anything.

More disappointed than she cared to admit at his abrupt departure, she threw her energies into getting up and out, jumping in the shower to a blast of warm water before wolfing down breakfast and heading off for the tube.

During her walk she thought back to the previous evening, and how things had seemed to be going so well. Or had gone so well. That was until the text messages and his disappearing act.

Maybe he'd also overslept and had rushed for the train before being able to send a message.

Upon entering the station, she grabbed a copy of the London Daily Post and headed for the platform, shoulder to shoulder with the other morning commuters.

She was still thinking of Ruben as the train set off - by now convincing herself that it had been a one night stand, and she should expect the cold shoulder treatment from Ruben. She would have to change her habits, grab a coffee from the stall just outside the station, maybe pass on the snacks, which would do her good anyway.

She should have known that someone as handsome and self-assured as Ruben would be trouble.

The whole date to watch him perform was probably a well-worn seduction technique.

How could she have thought he would really be interested in her?

As the train screeched and jerked onwards on its journey towards central London, she directed her anger at herself, flushing crimson at the thought of how she had offered herself up to be another notch on someone's belt.

What an idiot.

In an attempt to distract herself from her increasingly self-destructive thoughts, she buried herself in the newspaper, although even the celebrity gossip columns reminded her of Ruben, as she couldn't banish his voice making comment on the worth of what she was reading.

She got to the Secret Crush page.

And that is when everything changed.

Brown haired beauty on the Edgware to Euston tube each morning, with your cool red shoes, stripy tops and gorgeous smile. You brighten my day in so many ways! I'm the shy guy who shares your carriage. Want to share more than a commute?

Olivia re-read the message, her heart beating faster.

Was this really directed at her?

The tube route, the hair colour, the red shoes, the stripy tops she often favoured wearing, it all matched.

She stole a glance around the carriage. The train had got busier with each station, as usual, and it was now packed. So from her seated position, with people standing all around her, it wasn't easy to see who else was in the carriage. But still she tried to spot anyone who might be looking at her, watching for a reaction, or trying to make a connection.

And then she realised that she wasn't on her usual train, so this person, whoever they were, wouldn't be here anyway.

She read the message for the third time, as if on this next occasion it would suddenly become obvious that it wasn't in fact about her at all. But she felt certain that it must be directed at her.

She felt uncomfortable, even though it was highly unlikely that this person, whoever they may be, would be on this later train.

Unless they were stalking her.

Olivia dropped her eyes down into the newspaper, wishing that she hadn't just thought of that scenario. It was funny really, she loved reading these messages, and had never seen them as anything more than romantic gestures; if sometimes a little on the hopeless side. But now she might be the focus, it all of a sudden took on a more sinister perspective, and the anonymous message felt threatening.

And then she had a thought that made her feel a lot better.

Maybe the message was from Ruben.

Yes, that was probably it. Why hadn't she thought of it straight away? He'd probably sent in the message to the paper before they'd arranged their date. Now she smiled as she read the message again with Ruben's voice.

Thank goodness for that.

OLIVIA RESISTED the temptation to speak to Ruben as soon as she arrived at work. In truth, she was still unsure about how he felt about the previous night's events, and needed a little more time to consider what she might say to him.

Also, she didn't want to appear too keen.

Her resistance lasted only until the mid-morning break. The first hour and a half of the morning had been difficult to focus, and she needed answers if she was going to have any chance of getting through her lengthening to-do list.

She took an order for a flat white and a coffee and walnut muffin from Katherine, before heading downstairs to find out where she stood.

But as she took a steadying breath and turned the corner into the cafe, Ruben wasn't there.

'Hi,' Clive said, another of the cafe's employees, a friendly guy who must have been past retirement age. 'The usual?' he said. 'You're a little later today.'

'It was a bit of a rush this morning,' she replied, looking behind into the small kitchen area for any signs of Ruben. He could have been preparing the lunchtime meals. But there was no sign of him. 'Yes, the usual please, plus a flat white.'

Clive nodded and turned to make the drinks.

'Is Ruben not in today?' she asked.

'Called in sick,' he replied, as he prepared the machine for the coffees.

'Oh,' Olivia said, not meaning to say it out loud.

Clive turned. 'You sound disappointed,' he noted. 'Can't say I blame you,' he smiled. 'I mean, he is a good looking lad. But I was in my time, too, honest.'

Olivia blushed. 'I...'

'Sorry,' he said. 'Just teasing. How rude of me. I should stick to making the coffees. You can get in trouble these days for making inappropriate comments. And probably quite right too. Some bad things used to be said in the workplace, back in the day.'

He turned back to continue the drinks.

'Is he okay?' Olivia questioned. 'Nothing serious?'

'Said he felt awful,' he said. 'Thought he might have some kind of virus.'

'You spoke to him?'

'He called me first thing, seeing if I could come in and cover.'

'What time?'

Now Clive looked confused, no doubt wondering why she was so interested in the details. But he answered anyway. 'About half past seven.'

So he'd called Clive sometime after he'd left her flat.

Maybe that's why he'd left, because he woke up feeling unwell.

But why wouldn't he have left a note to explain?

'I hope he's okay,' Olivia managed to say, 'I mean, there have been some nasty bugs going around in the past few weeks.'

'I'm sure he'll live,' Clive joked, placing the two coffees down on the counter.

Olivia paid for the coffees and muffins that she added to the order.

'Probably one of those twenty-four hour things', he added. 'So he might be better by this evening.'

'This evening?'

'Well he said he fell pretty ill last night, so he'll probably be okay tonight.'

23

Cullen called Sarah first thing in the morning, to explain the situation. He had already made the decision that he wouldn't now be returning up north that day, as planned. He needed to be here, to take forward the potential investigation. But he wanted Sarah's blessing, and he wanted to be able to explain.

The last thing he wanted was for another rift to develop between them.

Sarah was understanding if obviously disappointed at the news.

'It will just be a few days,' Cullen promised. 'Just long enough for me to determine whether this is actually our investigation or not. And if it is, I'll hand over to Danny and he can take things forward.'

'Are you sure you'll be able to resist the temptation?' Sarah replied.

Cullen knew just what she was getting at. Yes, it was difficult sometimes to let go of an investigation, to hand it to a colleague, but he trusted DI Lomax completely and knew that he would do a good job.

'I want to come back up to you as soon as I can,' he replied. 'I promise I won't be any longer than I have to.'

'I'll hold you to that,' she said.

'I'll prove it,' he said. 'The idea I had for Philip that I mentioned. Wigan Warriors have these special matchday experiences for people with dementia. Wigan's game with St Helens at the weekend, I'll contact the club first thing tomorrow, see if there's a space for me and Phil to go. If there is, I'll book it.'

'You don't need to prove anything to me,' Sarah said. 'And what if something doesn't go to plan this week? You might not be able to keep your promise. Even though you want to.'

'No, I'll be back,' he insisted. 'I'll give the club a ring and hopefully there'll be a space.'

~

CULLEN SHOWERED, before wolfing down a cooked breakfast in the hotel restaurant while reading the morning edition of the London Daily Post. They had a report on the events of the previous evening at Angel station, which they had cleverly headlined "Fallen Angel". The article didn't name Cullen as being involved, and had mostly used lines lifted from the brief British Transport Police press release that had gone out later that evening.

Fuelled up, he made his way over to police headquarters, in the hope that Chief Superintendent Maggie Ferguson was free. He would need to convince her to let him do these initial investigations when she had advised him to take some time off. And after what happened the previous week, he didn't dare to go behind her back.

It just wasn't worth the risk. She had warned him in no

one certain terms how close he had come to losing his job by disobeying her orders and he was in no mind to test her resolve on that score.

~

'I HEARD about last night's incident,' Maggie Ferguson said as Cullen began to explain about the situation that had found himself in the previous evening. 'That was fortunate, you being right in the vicinity,' she added with very dry wit.

'Yes, it was a strange coincidence,' he said. 'Not so fortunate for the lady in question.'

'Indeed,' she replied solemnly. 'I hear that she was a university researcher.'

'Yes,' he confirmed.

'So,' she said, 'Tell me about what happened, and how it affects us.'

Cullen explained the events, finishing off with the suspicions of the last witness that the girl had been scared of someone in the final minutes of her life.

Maggie Ferguson paused and thought as Cullen finished his account. 'And what are your instincts telling you?' she said finally.

'My instincts are telling me that she fell, but maybe she fell because of someone else.'

Maggie Ferguson nodded, considering the possibility. 'You don't think she jumped?'

'I don't think so,' he replied. The witnesses weren't sure, but from looking at the CCTV, it didn't seem to me that she jumped. Plus, if she had intended to kill herself, I think she would've waited until the train was closer. But what actually happened is that she fell when the train was far away enough to stop before an impact.'

'Maybe,' she replied. 'Or maybe she was so distraught that she didn't really think about the timing of the jump, she just waited until she could hear the train, and then did what she had to do. She didn't realise the train would be able to stop in time.'

'I don't think it was deliberate,' Cullen said, his opinion hardening as he listened to Maggie Ferguson's posed alternative explanations.

'So, if it was the case that someone was following her, and this resulted in her falling to her death, we've got quite a serious situation on our hands, haven't we?'

'Yes,' he agreed.

'We need to determine what happened as soon as possible,' she continued. 'If this does come under the jurisdiction of Operation Archangel, we need to know, and we need to know fast.'

'I agree.'

'Look, Paul,' she said. 'I'm going to save you the bother of asking, and say that I would like you to urgently take this forward and determine whether we believe what happened last night does indeed come under our jurisdiction. I'm sure that's what you were going to propose, wasn't it?'

'Yes, it was.'

'But,' she continued, 'I do feel it would be good form to work with the London team for the moment, until we know for certain what this is all about. It may well turn out to be suicide, or just an unfortunate accident with no sinister explanation, so it makes sense to keep this jointly led for the moment.'

'I agree,' Cullen said. He didn't tell Maggie Ferguson that

he had already called the London team to arrange a meeting at the British Transport Police National Railways CCTV Headquarters in just over two hours' time. He had also taken the liberty of phoning his friend Anthony Braddock, the lead of the CCTV unit, so his team could already start looking through the recordings.

It wouldn't have gone down well with her.

'So what are your plans?' she enquired.

'We need to take a closer look at the CCTV. We need to look at all the available cameras at Angel. If we can track the victim through the station, I'm hoping that if there is a perpetrator, we'll be able to identify them.'

Maggie Ferguson nodded her agreement. 'Well I suggest you do that as soon as possible, and ensure you invite a colleague from the London team to accompany you.'

Cullen maintained a poker face as his boss suggested the very actions that he had already initiated. 'Good idea,' he said.

24

Olivia returned to the office. She'd managed to suppress her surprise at the claim that Ruben had been taken ill the previous evening. He certainly hadn't shown any signs of illness during their time together.

Why had he lied?

'Here you go,' she said, handing the coffee and muffin to Katherine.

'You okay?' Katherine said, spotting something in Olivia's facial expression.

Olivia's reaction was enough to prompt her colleague to gesture for them to move into the small meeting office.

'Something wrong?' Katherine said, closing the door. Olivia looked through the windows at the back of Henry, who was deep in financial data analysis, listening to something on headphones.

'I had a date with Ruben last night,' Olivia revealed.

Katherine's mouth fell open in a characteristically over-the-top reaction. Then she smiled broadly. 'Wow, Olivia, good on you! That guy is hot!' She checked herself when remembering that Olivia wasn't exactly looking over the moon. 'Did it not go well?' she asked, her face now serious and counsellor-like.

'It went brilliantly,' Olivia replied. 'At least, I thought it had...'

'But now he's acting all weird?'

'What makes you say that?'

'Duh. Because he's a man,' she replied. 'That's what men do. Let me guess. You had a great time last night, everything went well.' She looked at her and smiled as if what she had just seen revealed something very interesting. '*Really* well. And then, this morning, he's gone all cool and aloof. Am I right?'

'Well, not exactly.'

'But I'm along the right lines?'

'Maybe,' Olivia admitted, again glancing outside at Henry and hoping to God that their conversation wasn't being heard in the main part of the office. It would be mortifying to know Henry was listening to this. But the office was always pretty soundproof, so it was highly unlikely he could hear anything.

'So what's happened?' She took a bite of her muffin and sat back, as if settling down to watch a movie.

'This morning I woke up and he'd already left the flat,' she said, now regretting starting to tell the story to Katherine. It would have been best just to put a brave face on things and deal with this herself, rather than opening up and becoming potential office entertainment. 'And I've just found out that he phoned in sick this morning.'

Katherine didn't look surprised. 'Like I said, that's what men do.'

Olivia didn't share Katherine's disdainful world view of the male sex.

'There might be an explanation,' she said.

But the facts spoke for themselves. At least based on current knowledge.

'Maybe,' Katherine said, humouring her. 'Have you tried to call him?'

'I haven't got his number,' she said.

'Oh.'

'I'd better get back to work,' Olivia said, wanting to cut the conversation now. She decided she definitely wasn't going to tell her about the Secret Crush message. She now was doubting that it was even about her at all.

'Sure.'

Olivia knew what Katherine would be thinking - that it was weird that they'd been on a date but didn't have one another's phone numbers. But it wasn't like he had refused to give it to her - the issue just hadn't come up.

'Let me know if you need to chat again,' she offered.

They exited the office and Olivia noticed that Henry had at some point during the past few minutes removed his headphones.

'Everything okay?' he asked, as she passed and caught his eye.

'Just some issue with one of the schools,' Katherine interjected, before Olivia could reply.

He nodded but didn't look convinced, and instead kept his eye on Olivia as she returned to her desk.

Then he clicked on the web browser and continued the task that he'd been rudely interrupted from completing.

It had just taken on an even greater importance.

'OLIVIA, WE NEED TO TALK.'

Olivia was shocked to hear Ruben on the other end of the work phone. When it had called through, just before lunchtime, she hadn't thought for a second that it would be him.

'Okay,' she said, conscious that everyone was in the office and would be in prime position to listen in. 'What about?'

'Not on the phone,' he said. 'This needs to be in person. I want to explain. It's time I told you the truth.'

25

Cullen arrived at the British Transport Police CCTV Headquarters just before eleven thirty. The building, newly opened just over a month ago, was home to what was undoubtably one of the British Transport Police's prime assets - access to the footage of tens of thousands of cameras across the national rail network, including comprehensive coverage throughout the London Underground.

Cullen had lost count of the number of cases that had hinged on the evidence from those recordings. It was a key difference that separated the work of the British Transport Police from the regular police forces. Yes, the other police forces did rely on CCTV images, but none to the extent of the BTP. Yet still, it was never a given that cases could be solved, or even partly explained, by video evidence. There was a range of factors that needed to be in place for the technology to be useful during any investigation.

Cullen glanced at his watch as he reached the building. The detective from the London division hadn't arrived yet. He didn't know which one of the team would have been sent to work with him, but he knew them all, and they were by and large a decent group of detectives. It didn't bother him that this part of the investigation at least would be shared with the regional force. It was something that they did all the time.

Cullen entered the building and reported to reception. He'd only been waiting at the seated area for a couple of minutes when Anthony Braddock, Lead of the CCTV hub, approached.

'Paul, how nice to see you again so soon,' Anthony said, shaking his hand as Cullen stood up to greet him.

'Always a pleasure,' Cullen replied. Anthony had been a useful contact ever since Cullen had arrived in the capital. He had helped him out on countless cases, including his escapades in the previous week.

'We are expecting someone from the regional team?' he said.

'Yes,' Cullen replied. 'Not sure who, but they're late. Had any luck?' Cullen ventured, as they both looked across to the doors hoping to see the other detective appear, so they could get on with business.

'There are some things for you to look at, when we go up,' Braddock replied.

Cullen smiled. Anthony always loved to build up the suspense, and he hadn't really expected him to open up this time.

'I'm glad things worked out for you last week,' Anthony said, changing the subject.

'Me too,' Cullen said. Anthony had been one of the first ports of call the previous week, during Cullen's hunt for Natalie Long. And although the CCTV images that they had viewed at Paddington station around the time that Natalie had disappeared did not reveal anything in particular, Cullen had been extremely grateful for the way that Anthony had supported him in his below the radar investigation. That was one reason why he had called him, to let him know the outcome. Cullen was conscious that everyone who helped at every stage during an investigation was important and worthy of recognition and respect. Some detectives used and abused their colleagues in the quest for the solving of a case, not looking back at those that aided them on their way, but this was not Cullen's mode of working.

'Hey, aren't you supposed to be on holiday this week?' Braddock said, suddenly remembering what Cullen said to him the previous week.

'Tony had a heart attack on Monday,' Cullen revealed. The Chief Super called me, so I came back home the next morning.'

'My goodness,' he said. 'Is he okay?'

Cullen nodded. 'Tony is doing okay. I was supposed to go back up north this morning, until the events of last night took me in a different direction.'

Anthony laughed to himself. 'I don't know, you detectives, you do seem to attract trouble.'

'Tell me about it,' Cullen agreed.

~

A FEW MINUTES LATER, Detective Inspector Marianne McGuire entered the building. The dark-haired Irish officer cast her eyes across to the two men and smiled a hello as she reported to reception.

Cullen was pleased to see DI McGuire. She was a good

detective, and they had got on well during a number of co-operative investigations over the past couple of years since she had arrived from her home country of Ireland.

The last time that they had worked together was on a particularly nasty gangland case, where they had been successful in identifying and tracking down a sinister figure who had been terrorising local young people into working for his drugs network. DI McGuire had really impressed him with her determination and work ethic. He had also enjoyed her dry, smart sense of humour, which was always welcome relief in their line of work.

It would however make handing over the case to DI Lomax that bit more problematic, given that he and DI McGuire had dated for a time the previous year. According to DI Lomax, it was a mutual decision to end the relationship, but the look in his colleague's eyes told a different story. Cullen had never asked him to elaborate further, and he hadn't mentioned it to Marianne either.

Policing was complicated enough without adding intimate relationships into the mix.

'DCI Cullen, good to see you,' Marianne said in her soft Southern Irish accent, approaching with her warm smile and bright green eyes. 'I heard that you were quite busy last week.'

'I see the word got around.'

'Oh yes,' she said, 'it was quite the talk of the office. You have a new nickname.'

'Oh?'

'Liam Neeson,' she smiled.

He got the joke immediately. It was a reference to Neeson's character in the film *Taken*, where the leading man undertook a vigilante mission against those who had kidnapped his daughter.

He actually quite liked the nickname, although he wasn't going to admit it here.

'Nobody messes with my daughter,' he couldn't help but say.

26

'It's time I told you the truth,' Ruben said. He gestured to the bench just off to their left, which a young family had just vacated. He'd asked her to come over to the park, just a few minutes' walk from the office. 'Let's take a seat over there.'

They made their way side-by-side and sat down, looking out over the lake. The silence was only for a matter of half a minute, maybe less, but for Olivia it felt like much longer.

Ruben looked to make a couple of false starts, before the words came. 'This is really difficult for me to talk about,' he began. 'So you'll have to just bear with me. Okay?'

'Okay,' Olivia replied, wondering with some trepidation what this was all about. The calm, assured Ruben who she knew, or thought she knew, had been replaced by someone who was skittish, their face ashen.

Could whatever he was trying to tell her be so bad?

'The other night, at the open mike, you asked me if I'd ever been in a band.'

'Yes.'

'I said I hadn't. But that was a lie.'

'Okay...'

He was still looking out towards the lake, his focus seemingly on the swans that were off to their right, circling gracefully on the shimmering, sun-drenched waters.

'I was in a band, called Fallen Heroes. We formed at high school, when we were fourteen. There were four of us - me, Nick, Matt and Julian. I was the singer and lead guitarist, Nick played the bass, Matt the keyboard and Julian on drums. We played rock, mostly covers at first, for our own enjoyment. And then we started to play at parties, weddings, some business events. We started to write our own songs, and played those too. We put them out on social media - we'd built up quite a following by now - and things really started to take off. Suddenly we were playing venues in the towns and cities for people, fans, who were coming to hear us, our music. We toured across New Zealand, even appeared on TV.'

'That's amazing,' Olivia said gently, wary of misreading the mood and injecting too much positivity into what was still a noticeably sombre account.

He smiled tightly. 'Yes, it was amazing. And it got better. We were contacted by a record company in Australia. One of their scouts had been over and happened to see one of our gigs. They liked what they saw, and invited us to fly over to Sydney to discuss options.'

'Wow.'

He nodded. 'We were all so excited. We were only seventeen. So we got on the plane, business class. They put us up in an amazing hotel in downtown Sydney, looking out over the Opera House. It was like nothing I'd stayed in before. It felt like we were in Wonderland, you know? The next day, we met with the record executives. We played an acoustic gig in front of their team, at the top of their building on a garden terrace, which went really well. We spent the rest of the day touring the city, seeing all the sights, doing the open top tour and all that. And the next day they called us back into the office and offered us a record deal.'

'That must have been so exciting.'

'It was, it really was. A two album deal. But there was more. They wanted us to support Golden Son on the Australian leg of their world tour. You know the band?'

Olivia nodded. 'Of course. I think they've had a couple of hits here.'

'They're big, particularly in Australia, where they come from. I mean, to support them was a huge step up for us. They were playing in the big football stadiums, all over the country - Sydney, Melbourne, Perth, Brisbane. All over the place. The biggest venue we'd played at until then was a five hundred seater, but these places were for tens of thousands.'

'The record company must have really believed in you,' Olivia noted.

'They did. And so did we. I mean, we were never over-confident, but we believed in ourselves. We had that self-belief that I think you need in life, to really live your best life.'

Olivia was listening, but she was now also playing through the scenarios in her head as to why this apparently very positive story might have turned sour.

Maybe the tour had to be cancelled.

Maybe the record company went out of business.

Or maybe the band had fallen out and broken apart just on the cusp of their big break?

'And then...'

But as Olivia watched Ruben's voice faltering, and his face twitch, she doubted it was anything so mundane. This was more than a budding music career gone up in smoke, surely.

'And then everything changed,' he said, spluttering out of the words as if he was coughing up something horrible. 'Everything changed.'

'What happened?'

'I'm sorry, I can't,' Ruben said. 'I can't do this.' He almost fell off the bench, stumbling across the grass, before righting himself and setting off away from her with a quick stride.

Olivia started off after him. 'Ruben!' she said. 'Ruben, come back, it's okay.'

Except she didn't know if it was okay, because she didn't know what the hell this was all about.

Except that it was something bad.

Something very bad.

She jogged up to his shoulder. 'Please, just talk to me. I'm here to listen.'

He slowed his pace and came to a stop in the middle of the grass, his resistance to her request much less than she had imagined.

Facing one another, Olivia took his hands. 'It's okay, please, I know you want to tell me whatever is the matter.'

He was struggling to keep it together.

Struggling to hold back the tears.

'Just let it out,' she said.

He looked directly at her, his eyes almost pleading.

'I killed them,' he said finally. 'I killed my friends.'

27

Olivia watched Ruben's face crumple as she withdrew her hands from his. She had the urge to turn and run, not wanting to find out any more, but managed to stand her ground.

'It was an accident,' he said, his face pleading, 'a terrible accident. But it was my fault.'

Olivia looked around. They were in the middle of the grass, with no-one within hearing distance, but it still felt too public for a conversation like this.

However she also didn't want to be alone with him any more.

He sat down on the grass. 'Please, Olivia, I really need to tell you what happened. I need you to know the truth.'

She joined him.

'Only if you want to,' she said.

'I do want to. I do.'

He steadied himself, wiping tears from his face with the back of both hands.

'It was the fourth date of the tour, in Melbourne. Things

were going so well. Amazingly well. We'd just done our best ever support slot to a sell-out crowd at the Melbourne Cricket Ground. We were buzzing. Totally buzzing. We went out to celebrate, downtown. I wasn't drinking, because I was on steroids for an injury to my ankle I'd done at the last concert, so I decided I'd drive the guys to and from our hotel into the city. We'd hired out an open-top Porsche to cruise around the area while we were there. It became a kind of ritual each time we were in a new city, to hire out a supercar of someone's choice, just for a couple of days.'

Olivia listened without interrupting, her mind still hearing those words, over and over again, like a warped mantra.

I killed them. I killed my friends.

'We went around some of the bars, then hit a club, stayed there until the early hours. Then on the drive back it happened.'

He gazed at her with pained eyes.

'It was almost three in the morning. We were all tired, I guess, but I didn't realise just how tired I was. It was okay where there were streetlights, but once we hit the unlit roads, I started to feel awful. The next thing I remembered was hearing the emergency services, trying to bring me round. I was wedged underneath the steering wheel, and had hit my head against the side of the car, but apart from that I wasn't seriously injured. But the others...'

'They all died?'

'At the scene,' he confirmed. 'All three of them. The car had hit the side of a bridge, the left hand side taking much of the impact. Julian had been in the front passenger seat and took the full force. His face was...' He shook his head and pinched his nose hard. 'His face was unrecognisable. The other two, Matt and Nick, they hadn't been wearing seatbelts, the force of the impact was too much – they were thrown out into the road.'

'It was an accident,' Olivia found herself saying, as she placed a hand on his knee.

He shook his head. 'I should have told them how I was feeling,' he said. 'I should have stopped the car, and taken a break, pulled in to an all-night garage for a coffee.'

'If you'd thought this would have happened, you would have done that, of course you would.'

'Oh, yes, hindsight is a wonderful thing,' he said bitterly.

Olivia hesitated before asking the question. 'What happened after that?'

'The police investigation came first. I was breathalysed, checked for drugs, questioned about how I ended up driving a high end sports car into a bridge. Of course I came back clear - no alcohol or drugs in my system. Just a heavy dose of guilt. I didn't tell the police how tired I'd been feeling before the crash. I stuck to the line that one minute I was driving, the next I'd crashed, with no memory of what happened in between. Next came the families. They believed me too. Treated me as one of their own. Made me the guest of honour at their sons' funerals.'

'It must have been so awful.'

'It was. But I deserved it, Olivia. I really did deserve it all.'

'You're being too harsh on yourself.'

'I tried to pick myself up, get on with my life in New Zealand. But the memories were everywhere, inescapable, haunting me, so I decided I needed to leave.'

'And that's when you volunteered in Nepal?'

'Yes. I signed up for the charity work. It felt like the right thing to do. I could help others, while also leaving my old life behind. I did that for three years, living up near the Himalayas. It was so good. I should have stayed there. But I wanted to challenge myself again, and saw the opportunity to do a funded PhD in London. I applied, didn't expect to get it, but when I did, it just felt like the right thing to do.'

'That all sounds very understandable,' Olivia said. She looked carefully at Ruben, and wanted to raise him up from his despair. He'd been through an extremely traumatic experience, one that had dramatically changed his life's trajectory, and despite all that he had achieved both before and after the event in Melbourne, he obviously still hadn't escaped its horror.

'I felt like I was starting to put it all behind me after I arrived in London,' he said, as if reading her mind. 'Nepal was wonderful, but I still felt as though I was just hiding away from my real self, and my life. But here, in London, it really did feel like a fresh start. It's such an amazing city, so diverse, you can be anyone you want to be, and do anything. You can leave the past behind. I felt reborn, that I had a second chance. I even started to play the guitar again. I hadn't picked up an instrument since the crash. That was a mistake.'

'A mistake? What do you mean?'

He smiled ruefully. 'Because of what happened last night.'

~

'I HADN'T INTENDED to start doing the music slot, but one night at the pub I got talking to one of the guys behind the bar, and he told me they were starting an open mike the next week. They were asking around their customers, to see if anyone fancied kicking things off.'

'So you decided to do it?'

'Yes. Instinctively, I mentioned that I played guitar, and he begged me to sign up - said he'd been struggling all week to get anyone to do it. I said no at first, but it was really tempting, just to have that feeling of playing in front of people again. So later in the evening, when he asked again I guess I couldn't resist. I didn't think it could do any harm. It was just one night.'

'But it wasn't just one night,' Olivia stated, remembering how the big crowd in the pub seemed to have come to see him.

'No, it wasn't just one night. I did the slot the following week, and it went well. There was only me and one other guy, who to be honest wasn't that great. The pub wasn't that busy, but the people in there seemed to really like what I did. So did the manager of the place. He asked me to play again the following week.'

'So that's how you got the regular slot.'

'I couldn't resist agreeing. I'd forgotten how good it felt to perform in front of a crowd.' His eyes were blazing. 'I mean, you just can't beat that feeling, of people watching you, enjoying what you're doing, putting them under your spell. It's addictive, it really is. It's like a drug. That's how bands perform and perform and perform, the same songs, again and again. It's not for the money, at least not mostly. It's for the adrenalin, the thrill of it all.'

'All those people last night at the pub, they were there to see you?'

'After the second week, the numbers in the pub had gone up noticeably. The manager told me that people had come in asking about the Kiwi guy on the guitar, if he was performing that night. Word had got around. I checked social media, and people had been sharing it on Twitter. I should have known then that it had gone too far, that it was too risky and inviting trouble. But I just couldn't stop. By now I'd set up my Just Giving page, and the sets were bringing in a decent amount for the charity. I didn't want to stop. So I convinced myself that everything was going to be alright. I mean, I was thousands of miles away from home, and it had been a few years since our success in Australia. We were old news, from far away.'

Olivia now thought she knew what had happened. 'The girl at the bar, Stephanie. You said you'd known each other back in New Zealand.'

Ruben nodded. 'Yes,' he said flatly. 'We knew one another.'

'So what's the story?'

He hesitated, evidentially wondering what to say and how to say it.

'I met Stephanie Taylor in Melbourne, on the night of the crash,' he replied, finally. She was with a group of friends, in the first pub that we visited, and we got talking at the bar. They'd been to the concert. She recognised me, but said it was the first time she'd heard of the band, and had been there for the headliners, Golden Sun. I found out later that was a lie.'

'How so?'

'We chatted for a while at the bar,' he said, dodging the question for now, 'got on well, but the lads wanted to move on to the next place, so we said goodbye. She was pretty, you know, but I must admit I didn't think anything of it until I bumped into her again at the club.'

Olivia just listened, waiting for a punchline.

'I was watching the guys on the dance floor - my ankle was hurting again - and all of a sudden she came up behind me, a hand on my back, and we chatted some more. I was sober because of driving, although felt quite drunk with tiredness, but she was pretty gone, and much more flirty than earlier. We kissed and she wanted to come back to the hotel. I was really tempted, but then while she went to the bathroom, the guys came over and warned me off. One of her friends had spoken to them, telling them that they were only fifteen and she was a super fan of the group.'

'Oh.'

'Oh, indeed.'

'So what happened?'

'I tried to extricate myself from the situation, but she took it really badly, started to shout at me for leading her on. She was really angry, from the drink mostly, and I think she was embarrassed when I mentioned her age. Honestly, I couldn't calm her down, and people in the club were noticing. The guys decided we should leave, that it would be bad for publicity, but she followed me out of the club and kept the argument going in the car park. She was relentless. We got into the car and she was thumping on the windows, kicking the tyres. I was worried she was going to damage the car, or herself, so I just got out of there as soon as I could. She actually tried running after us, and nearly caught us at the lights around the corner, but I put my foot down.'

'And then the crash.'

Ruben looked at Olivia, sensing that she was working this out for herself. 'Everyone was on edge,' he said, slowly. 'I mean, the three others had been drinking, so they were hyped up already, but I was too, I was shaking, I could hardly hold the steering wheel. We started arguing. Julian was next to me, and he said I needed to be more careful, that I'd put the future of the band at risk by being with an underage girl, and creating a scene. Matt was already going through social media to see if anyone had posted footage. I told them it hadn't been my fault, but it boiled over, and I got angry and distracted...'

He trailed off.

'You didn't fall asleep,' Olivia said simply.

'No,' Ruben replied, after a pregnant pause. 'I didn't. I lied to the police, to all the families, maybe even to myself for a time.'

'Why?'

'Because I was afraid,' he replied. 'I thought if I told the police what had really happened, that we'd been arguing, that I might be charged with dangerous driving, and I might go to jail. I told the lie at the scene of the crash, while they were cutting me out, and I stuck to it. The other three people who really knew what happened were dead, so it was just my secret to keep.'

'Does no-one else know what really happened?'

'One other person,' he said. 'Stephanie Taylor. And now she's back in my life.'

'I DON'T UNDERSTAND, how did Stephanie find out what really happened?' Olivia asked.

Ruben laughed bitterly. 'Some idiot told her.'

'Why?'

He shook his head, and looked off towards the distance, as if searching for an answer among the surrounding parkland. 'I didn't mean to,' he said. 'But it happened.'

'I don't understand.'

'The weeks after the crash, they were a blur, and they

were awful,' he said. 'I stayed in Australia during the initial police investigation - the record company paid for my hotel - but it was a bad decision. I should have gone straight home to New Zealand, like my parents wanted me to. I felt so alone, yet I didn't want to have to face my family, not straight away. I had to get things straight in my head. But I just hid away in the hotel room, wallowing in guilt, self-pity and fear. By the third day, I started to panic, that the police would find out what really happened. They kept asking questions, details about the lead up to the crash, the same questions over and over again, as if they didn't believe me. It was like they knew more about what had happened, and I wondered whether someone who had been at the club had been talking. I felt like I really needed to find out if that was true.'

'You went to see Stephanie Taylor?'

'I tracked her down via Facebook,' he said. 'It wasn't difficult to find her profile. I offered to meet up, downtown, and she accepted. It was another terrible mistake.'

'What happened?'

He laughed ruefully. 'I meant to just find out about what she remembered about the night - she was pretty drunk, like I said, so I thought it was very likely that she hadn't remembered anything well, and knowing that would put my mind at rest. But she had remembered everything. She apologised for the argument, saying it had all just got out of hand, and that she was really sorry for what had happened afterwards. On the surface, the conversation was going well, but underneath, I was starting to panic. It turned really sour when I asked her outright if she had been talking to the police. She said she had. And then she smiled. She said: "But don't worry, I didn't tell them everything."'

'What did she mean by that?'

'What do you think? I felt totally sick to my stomach, I just didn't know what to do. And that's when I decided the best option, the only option, was to keep her close, keep her on side. I'd started the lie, and I had to keep it up, otherwise it would end up even worse for me.'

'So what did you do?'

'I said thank you to her. Then I apologised and said I wanted to make a fresh start for us both.'

'A fresh start? A relationship?'

'Yes.'

'But she was underage,' Olivia remembered. 'She was fifteen.'

'I know,' he said tightly. 'I was desperate. And I wasn't thinking properly.'

Olivia shook her head at the thought of this young girl being taken advantage of.

'So what happened?' she managed to ask.

'We went back to the hotel,' he said.

'No.'

'I know how it seems,' he said, on the defensive. 'I look back at it now and am ashamed, I really am, honestly.'

Olivia couldn't bring herself to reply directly to that. 'And then what?'

'We saw one another every day for the next few weeks, while I was in Melbourne - she lived there with her parents, although she was careful to ensure that they didn't know about us. Then I went back for the funerals in New Zealand, and when I decided to stay there, we kept up a long distance relationship before I let things fizzle out over the next few months.'

'You ghosted her?'

'No,' he said. 'I ended it, gently, you know, without really ending it.'

'And how did she feel about it?'

'I think she wanted to make it work,' he replied. 'But she was happy to stay friends, I think.'

'And did you?'

'What?'

'Stay friends?'

'It was difficult being back home,' he said, not answering the question. 'Everything reminded me of the guys, and what had happened. So six months after I returned, I went to Nepal, volunteering in the north of the country, on the edge of the Himalayas. I just wanted to leave my old life behind, and that included everything and everyone that had been part of it. I dropped off social media, didn't reply to calls and texts, made myself invisible. After a few weeks there, no-one from my old life was making contact with me anymore. And it was amazing. I was reborn. I should have never left.'

Olivia took a deep breath. Now was the time to ask about the text messages.

'I saw the messages she sent you last night.'

'I thought you might have done.'

'What did she mean?'

'She wanted to break us up,' he said. 'She couldn't stand seeing us together. Look, I'm really sorry I just walked out on you this morning. It was really rude of me. But seeing her, it really spooked me, and I had to get my head straight.'

'It's okay,' Olivia replied. 'I can see that.'

He reached out and took both her hands. 'Give me a second chance, Olivia. And let's leave the past where it belongs.'

28

Cullen and Marianne accompanied Anthony Braddock up to the third floor and through into the main CCTV control room. It was just one week since Cullen had been here, that time with his daughter Amy, as they had searched fruitlessly for sight of her friend Natalie Long at London's Paddington station.

This time he hoped for better news, and his spirits had been lifted by the mood of Braddock - he definitely seemed positive and that he was waiting for some kind of big reveal.

'This is Gary,' Braddock said as they entered the room. 'He is one of my senior analysts here at the hub. Been working for the past few hours to track down your lady, and whoever might have been following her.'

Cullen shook Gary's hand. 'Nice to meet you.' Gary smiled and again Cullen's hopes rose at his apparent positivity.

Surely he wouldn't look so happy if they had come up with nothing?

'Do take a seat,' Braddock directed. 'We've got all of the images ready, so please do sit back and enjoy the show.'

Braddock was always a bit too enthusiastic about the technology at his disposal. He was like a boy with new toys at the moment, given the fact that the place had only been open for just over a month and as he told him just last week, the kit was a big step up from what he had been used to in the old offices down near Vauxhall.

Cullen watched as Gary took to the controls, which were below a bank of screens running across the top of the wall.

'We tracked Emily from the entrance,' Gary explained, 'through the ticket hall, down the escalators and onto the platform. Of course, you've already seen the footage from the platform itself. But we do have a few things of interest from the other cameras, both towards ground level and also down on the platform edge.'

Cullen dared to hope that there might well be a breakthrough. Maybe this was one of those times where the cameras would do the work for them.

They watched as Gary played through the first set of footage. Cullen could see Emily enter and move towards the ticket gates. The camera then switched to the escalators, but once again Emily was in shot. The series of cameras followed her down to the platform level, where it then picked her up on the platform itself. But unlike the footage that he'd seen the previous evening, this camera was from the far side, looking towards the incident.

Cullen watched as in the near distance, Emily moved towards the small group of people at the platform edge. And then, just a few seconds later, she dropped onto the tracks. He was disappointed to find that the new viewing angle offered up nothing new, no hint of whether the fall had been deliberate or not.

'As you can see,' Braddock said, 'the additional camera angle is not conclusive at all, in terms of what led to the lady's fall.'

'The person in the baseball cap,' DI McGuire stated.

Cullen had seen them too. The individual had been in each shot. Not right behind their target, but a few people behind. Close enough.

'I'll play the footage through again,' Braddock said, not acknowledging DI McGuire's statement just yet.

THEY WATCHED the video play through again. This time all eyes were on the man coming up from behind Emily. He was some metres away, alongside others, and his behaviour up to the tragic incident was certainly nothing out of the ordinary.

But this all changed.

Cullen scrutinised the individual as they slowed their pace, but continued to close the gap between themselves and Emily. The baseball cap was pulled down low over their face, and there was no chance of the ceiling-mounted cameras capturing any of their facial features.

The person had come within a matter of metres as Emily turned briefly towards him before moving through the huddle of people at the platform edge.

A few seconds later she was on the tracks.

Cullen continued to watch the figure in the cap. While the other people around reacted in a way one would expect, given the horrific happening they had just witnessed, the man in the cap certainly did not do so.

The man stood there for a few short seconds, his face still shielded, but then simply turned and walked away. Cullen watched him stride away from the scene, a determined and focussed individual among the shock and panic.

He turned left towards the exit.

'I can see what you mean,' Braddock said finally, as the individual of their attention disappeared from shot. 'The guy in the baseball cap. His behaviour seemed pretty....odd.'

'Odd indeed,' Cullen agreed. 'What do you think?' he asked DI McGuire.

'Looks like he was following her. Do you think so, too?'

'Could well have been,' Cullen replied, thinking back to what one of the witnesses had said about Emily looking anxious in those moments before she fell. 'We shouldn't jump to conclusions though,' he added, as a note of caution. 'We're watching this through just one lens. Can we watch the whole thing through again, Anthony?'

'Of course,' he replied. 'We'll work forwards again, down to the platform.'

Gary nodded and switched the view to the ticket hall. 'Ready?'

Cullen nodded. 'Go ahead.'

They watched again as Emily appeared in shot, before touching in with her card at the barriers. Cullen trained his eyes to her left, waiting for the moment when the man in the baseball cap would surely appear.

'There he is,' Marianne stated.

Yes, there he was. There was just one person between him and Emily through the gates. But still, from the camera's vantage point, and the cap, there was no view of his face.

'The camera now switches to the escalators,' Braddock explained. Again the view was frustratingly obscured by the cap. But the man was visible, now two people in between him and Emily in front.

Cullen watched to see if Emily was behaving strangely; if there were any signs of the anxiety that had been mentioned.

Not until she reached the bottom of the escalator, heading for the platform. A camera just caught her glance to her left, just as she was passing through the archway to the platform.

Directly towards the person in the cap.

They were eye to eye.

'You see that too,' Marianne said.

'Yes,' Cullen replied. 'That is the moment.'

The moment - the split second that can transform the direction of a case, and shape the whole investigation.

'But still no view of them,' Cullen added.

'I'm afraid not,' Braddock said. 'They've got that cap on pretty tight. The rest of the footage is what you've already seen, from one of the platform's other cameras,' Braddock explained. 'Do you want to see it again?'

'Might as well,' Cullen said. 'For completeness sake. And DI McGuire here hasn't seen it yet.'

They watched the platform footage that Cullen had viewed at Angel's control room. Cullen tried to look for something different, anything that he might have missed.

'There is another look-back,' Marianne said, just as Emily had reached the far end of the platform. 'Not that obvious, but I'm sure there was.'

Cullen nodded. 'She was checking if they were still following. Gary,' he said to Braddock's colleague, 'can you rewind and pause when I give the nod.'

'Sure,' Gary replied, already bringing the recording back. 'Play from here?'

'Yes,' Cullen confirmed.

The recording started as Emily was nearing the group at the platform edge.

'There,' Cullen said.

The image froze with Emily's head turned ever-so-slightly, but significantly, towards her left.

Cullen exchanged a look with DI McGuire, who nodded.

'Can we get a zoom in of the person in the cap?' Cullen asked.

'We can,' Braddock said, hesitantly, 'but it might not tell us much from that distance.'

Gary highlighted the figure in the baseball cap with a selection square, before zooming in with a few taps of the control panel.

Cullen was disappointed that the close up didn't yield any identifying features. He'd hoped that the baseball cap might yield something, maybe a team logo, maybe a brand. But it was just dark.

'Can you get us some more close up shots, Anthony, track this guy through the station? And if you can also get any footage from outside the station, that would be particularly helpful.'

'Of course,' he said. 'No problem whatsoever. If you give us an hour, we'll pull out all the footage we can get, look at any close-ups that might be more useful than this, absolutely no problem.'

Cullen rose to stand. 'Much appreciated, Anthony.'

Braddock looked at his watch. 'Like I said, give me an hour,' he looked at his watch for a second time, 'maybe forty-five minutes, it will be ready and waiting for your perusal.'

'Thank you.' Cullen turned to Marianne. 'I'm sure we can find somewhere to hang out for the time being. Let's grab something to eat while we wait. We can talk things through. The staff canteen?' he suggested.

'Closed,' Braddock said apologetically. 'Flood yesterday.'

Cullen raised an eyebrow.

'Burst pipe, place was like a paddling pool by all accounts,' Braddock elaborated. 'You can always have a drink and wait in my office. I've got a kettle and tea bags.'

'I know a good place down the road,' Marianne interjected, just as Cullen was about to say yes to Braddock's offer.

'Costa?' Cullen joked.

'If you like,' she smiled. 'But I know another place. They do a great Irish coffee. Not that I'm being at all stereotypical, you understand.'

'To be sure,' Cullen smiled. 'Sounds good.'

29

'It's Olivia, isn't it?'

'Yes,' Olivia said warily, as the girl Ruben had introduced her to at the open mike session approached her. Olivia had just a few minutes before said goodbye to Ruben at the park, and was almost back at the office.

Had Stephanie been watching them?

'Stephanie,' she said, holding out a hand while shielding her eyes against the sun. 'We met at the pub.'

'I remember.'

She looked behind Olivia, as if checking out the land for hidden dangers. 'I wanted to be sure that you were on your own,' she explained.

'You mean without Ruben?'

She smiling knowingly. 'Something like that, yes. Can we go somewhere, you know, off the street?'

'Okay,' Olivia said, struck by the girl's jitteriness.

Surely it couldn't hurt to engage with her in a public place, and get her side of the story?

Although she was far from sure there was any future with

her and Ruben, it would be best all round if the situation between the three of them was resolved. She'd always hated unresolved conflict, so would try and make things right, even though it wasn't really her problem.

They retreated to a nearby coffee shop.

'How did you find me?' Olivia said, as they settled at a table with their drinks.

'I followed you both from the pub last night,' she admitted. 'I wasn't planning to, it was a gut reaction when I saw you leaving together. I needed to do something.'

'I don't understand.'

'I wanted to be able to get in contact with you,' she explained, 'and the best way of doing that was to find out where you lived. And I knew he wouldn't take you back to his place. From your address I got your name, and then your place of work.'

Olivia blushed slightly at the thought of a stranger knowing her private business.

She must have been watching the whole way home.

As they linked arm in arm.

The nervous conversation on the doorstep of the flat.

And the first kiss.

'I know this might all sound a bit freaky,' the girl admitted, 'and I wouldn't blame you for wondering what the hell this is all about. But that's why I'm here now, because you need to know the full facts.'

'I saw the texts that you sent to him,' Olivia revealed.

'Oh,' she said, shocked. 'You didn't ask him about them, did you?'

'Not at first. I didn't have the chance. He'd left my place early in the morning, before I could speak to him.'

'It spooked him,' she said, with a hint of pleasure.'

'But he told me just that you're trying to break us up.'

She shook her head. Then her face hardened. 'I shouldn't have sent those messages. I should have tried to speak to you, first. It was too risky to do what I did. I'm sorry.'

'Ruben explained,' Olivia revealed. 'He told me about what happened.'

'What?'

'He explained everything, just now.'

'What did he say?'

'He told me about the crash in Australia, what happened with his bandmates, and how you...' Olivia hesitated before going any further, for a second forgetting the role that Stephanie had played in the events. 'He explained about your relationship.'

She just laughed, shaking her head in disbelief. 'He used the story about the boyband?'

'The crash in Melbourne...'

'Where his three bandmates died?' she finished.

'Yes, but...'

'And I suppose I was the girl he met after the concert? The underage super-fan who argued with him in the nightclub, and then ran after the car?' she added, becoming more animated.

'Well, yes...'

'The girl who he dated afterwards, before he headed back to New Zealand for the funerals of his friends. The girl who he ghosted, before he headed off to India for his voluntary work?'

'Nepal, it was Nepal,' Olivia corrected.

'Oh, Nepal was it? Well, at least he's adding in a bit of variety there.'

Olivia was growing in her discomfort. 'Look, I really don't understand what the heck is going on here.'

This seemed to calm Stephanie down, make her see the situation from Olivia's point of view. 'You're right,' she said. 'Sorry, I know this is a lot to get your head around, and I'm probably not handling it the best. So maybe I'd better just cut to the chase.'

'Which is?'

'You're in danger.'

~

'I'M IN DANGER?' Olivia's skin prickled at the shocking revelation. 'In danger from Ruben?'

'Yes. Danger,' she reiterated.

'But, how?'

'What you've got to understand, is that everything, or virtually everything that guy has told you will be a lie.'

'What?'

'Ruben is a master manipulator,' she said. 'He's controlling, and abusive, psychologically.'

'That doesn't sound like...'

'I also think he's very probably a psychopath, but I don't know that for sure. I've read up about it, and he fits the description.'

Olivia put a hand to her head. 'This is...'

'Crazy?' Stephanie answered for her. 'Yes, it is crazy. But you've got to believe me. I'm warning you like someone else warned me.'

'You?'

'The whole story about the band, and the accident, and me, it's all a fiction,' she said. 'It never happened. At least not to him. He spun the same lies to me.'

'To you?'

'We were in a relationship,' she said. 'I met him at another open mike event, in Brixton. He was so charming and self-assured, and at the same time seemed to take a genuine interest in me. I really fell for him. It was going well for a while - really well, I thought. But then I began to realise he was gradually gaining more and more control over my life, what I was doing, what I was wearing, where I could go, who I could see. He was gaslighting me - making me question my sanity, swearing blind that he hadn't said the things he'd said, or did the things he'd done. My cat disappeared, and I'm certain he did something to her.'

'No.'

'He was never physically violent to me, but I do believe he hurt my cat. I know he did something. The day after my cat disappeared, he came over to my flat with her collar - said he'd found it while he was out putting up posters around the neighbourhood. I think he did it just to mess with me. He knew what had happened to her, I'm sure of it.'

'So, how did you...'

'Get out? Someone approached me, like I've approached you - a university researcher called Emily. Warned me about him, said that he'd done the same to her. It woke me up to what was happening. Gave me the clear sightedness to see the relationship for what it was; an increasingly abusive one.'

'But, if he was so controlling, how did you get away?'

'I got out of London,' she said. 'Took leave of absence from my job. Went to stay with my aunt in Cornwall for a few weeks. By the time I returned, he'd moved on.'

'To me?'

'I assume so. But maybe others too.'

'You bumping into him at the pub, was it by chance?'

'No. I didn't intend to ever see Ruben again, certainly didn't want to, believe me. But something weird happened. A friend of a friend on social media mentioned this guy who was performing at a pub in Edgware, and it was Ruben. I'm not sure why I went really. Maybe I wanted to show him that I wasn't afraid any more. Maybe I wanted to prove to myself that I wasn't afraid. But then I saw you with him, and I knew I needed to do something to warn you.'

'Then I get away, and he moves on to somebody else,' Olivia said.

Stephanie shrugged. 'I just wish there were a way of putting a stop to it.'

'There must be a way,' Olivia replied, a fire burning inside as she thought about all this man had done to countless women before her. 'This has to end here.'

PART IV

30

'So is this one of your regular haunts?' Cullen said, as they sat in the small pub that was just a short five minute walk from the CCTV Headquarters.

'One of them,' Marianne replied. 'It's owned by a family from Cork, they actually know my parents.'

'Well they do great Irish coffee,' he noted, enjoying the drink.

'I thought you'd approve.'

Cullen settled back and looked around the establishment. It was quiet enough for comfortable conversation away from others, but with enough of a buzz to prevent voices from carrying and being overheard.

'How's Danny?' Marianne asked suddenly. 'Doing okay?'

'He's okay,' Cullen replied, interested that she'd brought him up in discussion, and so quickly.

Was this why she had been so keen to meet outside of the CCTV building?

'Good,' she said, thinking of something. 'That's good. I'm glad he's doing well.'

'Look,' Cullen said, watching Marianne's face fall ever so slightly. 'Feel free to tell me to mind my own business, but what happened between you two?'

'Didn't Danny tell you anything?'

'Nothing directly,' he confirmed, 'but quite a lot indirectly.'

'I'm not sure I know what you mean?'

Cullen hesitated. He wondered whether he was going too far, speaking out of turn in a way that neither Marianne, and especially not Danny would appreciate.

'Indirectly?' she prodded.

Cullen blew out his cheeks. 'Danny isn't the kind of guy to open up about things like this,' he started. 'He likes to put on that bravado of his, you know what he's like, but since you two split, he's been different.'

'Different? In what way?'

Cullen chose his words carefully. He didn't want to say broken-hearted, even though that's exactly what it looked like from Cullen's perspective whenever Marianne's name had come up. In fact, he'd been quite taken aback by DI Lomax's reaction. 'Subdued,' he said finally.

'Subdued? Danny?'

'Yes. Subdued. Gutted, maybe.'

'Did he not tell you anything about what happened?'

'Only a little. And I mean a little. I asked him one day if he was alright, because he really wasn't himself, and he said that you two had split up the previous night. I made a comment about being surprised, because it had seemed to be going well. And he said: "So had I." Which I took to mean that it wasn't his decision to end things.'

Marianne was toying with the spoon in her drink. 'Well you'd be right,' she confirmed.

Cullen frowned. 'Then why do you look as gutted as he does about it all?'

'Because it was going well. Really well. And I didn't want to end it.'

Cullen shook his head. 'I'm not sure I understand young people any more,' he only half-joked. He certainly didn't understand his daughter at times.

'Well thanks for classing me as young,' she quipped.

'You're the right side of forty, and younger than me by ten years. But wiser than that,' he added.

'That's true,' she smiled.

'So you must have had good reason to do what you did.'

Marianne nodded. 'Yes, I did.' Although her expression told a different story.

'So what happened?'

'I found out something,' she said. 'About Danny. About what he'd been like in the past.'

~

CULLEN NOW THOUGHT he knew where this was going. 'You mean, being a bit of a ladies' man?' Danny had a reputation, and by all accounts, it was well-deserved. Good looking and charismatic, Cullen didn't need much imagination to see how DI Lomax might be able to play the field.

Marianne nodded. 'He's been with a lot of women, some married or in relationships. He's cheated on girlfriends. I really, I didn't, I don't want to be in a relationship with someone who can do that. I need to be able to trust them, totally.'

'I can understand that,' he said. 'I imagine most people would feel exactly the same.'

Marianne smiled tightly. 'My dad, he left us when I was ten. He was having an affair with a married woman, and ran off with her. Turns out it wasn't the first time he'd cheated on my mum. He'd been doing it from before they got married. She knew about it too - but she always forgave and took him back, after he promised it would never happen again. But it still did. And then, that day, two weeks before Christmas, he just upped and left. Didn't say goodbye. Not to me, my mum or my little brother, who was eight and adored him. He just disappeared. We never heard from him again.'

'I'm sorry to hear that,' Cullen replied. And he really was sorry. Sitting there, he could see the hurt, raw and unhealed, in her eyes.

She looked at him earnestly. 'I can't risk being involved with someone like that.'

'Danny isn't your father though,' he tried.

'Have you ever cheated on your wife?' She gazed at Cullen. 'Sorry,' she said, catching herself. 'I shouldn't have asked such a personal question, it was rude of me.'

'It's okay,' he said. 'I haven't.'

She nodded, as if her point had been proven. But she looked far from happy.

'How did you find out about Danny's past?' he asked.

'He told me.'

Cullen couldn't hide his surprise. 'He told you?'

'One night, we were watching a movie at his flat, and had just been out for a lovely meal. I felt so happy, so comfortable with him, so at ease. He'd asked about my family before, but I'd dodged the questions about my past. You see, I've hardly ever spoken about what happened with my dad, not even to some of my best friends - it's something that is so painful I just built that wall and kept people out. But that night, things felt so right that I decided it was time to let him in.'

'And he decided to do the same,' Cullen noted.

Marianne frowned. 'How do you mean?'

'He decided to let you in.'

This caused her to think hard. But then she shook her head. 'I appreciated his honesty, but it doesn't change the facts, that I can't be with someone who can do those kind of things.'

'Did those kind of things,' Cullen said.

'Once a cheater always a cheater,' she countered.

'Not necessarily,' he said. He didn't really know why he was defending DI Lomax so strongly. His actions in the past certainly were indefensible. He had hurt people again and again. But people could, and should, be able to change. And he'd seen how Danny had been with Marianne. Cullen didn't feel Lomax deserved to be punished for his honesty.

'But I couldn't be sure,' she said. 'I could never be sure he wouldn't do the same to me.'

'At some point you just have to trust the one you love.'

She let out an embarrassed laugh. 'I never said anything about love.'

'Just go with me on this one,' he said.

'Okay...'

'Look, he didn't have to tell you about his past, but he did. That says a lot, surely. He opened up to you, he must have known it was a risk, but he wanted to be honest. For him to do that, you must have meant a lot to him. What did he say after he told you?'

'That he'd changed since he met me, and that he would never dream of doing that sort of thing again.'

'And how did you respond?'

'I was shocked, and disappointed - totally gutted to be honest. I said I'd need time to think things through, and left. The next day I texted him and ended it.'

'And that was that?'

'He texted me back, reiterating that he'd changed, and he was sorry for the past. I never replied.'

'It's still not too late to reply. It's never too late to try and save something good.'

She thought some more. 'You're impressive,' she said at last. 'I never knew you were so insightful about relationships.'

Now it was his turn to laugh away the embarrassment. 'Believe me, Sarah would not agree with you on that one.'

'Is...Danny seeing anyone?' she ventured.

'As far as I know, he hasn't been in a relationship since you two broke up. At least that's what he told me.'

'Oh. Neither have I.'

'Sounds like you two need to get together,' he said. 'I think you've got unfinished business. Speaking of which,' he said, wanting to now change the subject, 'what are your thoughts about what we've seen so far?'

'You're right, let's get back down to business, Marianne said, sitting up straighter. 'It seems pretty clear to me that Emily was being followed, by the person of interest in the cap.'

'And do you think she jumped?'

'Fell,' she replied, without hesitation. 'In her desperation and panic to get away.'

Cullen nodded. 'I think so too. Looking at the videos, it seems clear to me that the person in the cap was following her, and she knew it.'

'I just hope Braddock comes up with something,' Marianne noted.

'So do I. But I doubt it.'

'Really?' she replied, surprised at his pessimism.

Cullen shrugged. 'Whoever this person is, they seemed to be very careful in shielding their face. I think they knew full well where the cameras were. So I very much doubt they will have let their guard slip.'

'Maybe the roadside cameras?' she offered.

'It's probably the best chance we've got, but I would be surprised. This individual knew what they were doing.'

THEY MADE their way back to CCTV Headquarters, where Cullen's suspicions were unfortunately confirmed to be correct.

'I'm afraid it's not great news,' Anthony Braddock announced as he accompanied them back up to the hub. 'We've been through the videos and zoomed in, but none of the images reveal any additional information that could be helpful for identification purposes. I'm sorry.'

'And the roadside cameras?' Cullen asked.

Braddock shook his head. 'We have got shots of the person as they enter the station, shortly after Emily enters, but again, the cap is obscuring the face.'

'Can we take a look at the roadside one?' Cullen said. 'Just for completeness.'

'Sure.'

The video played through, and as Braddock had explained, it added nothing extra.

It was frustrating, but no surprise.

Cullen and Marianne said their goodbyes and reconvened on the street outside.

'So, next step her family and friends?' Marianne said.

Cullen nodded. 'Find out if she's mentioned anything about being followed. Or if there are any relationship issues in her recent history. There's a good chance that she might have said something to someone, if this is something that has been going on for some time.'

'And if it was just a random incident?' Marianne asked.

'Then we've got very little to go on. And that worries me.'

'Me too.'

31

Olivia had to get back to work, so she swapped numbers with Stephanie and they promised to keep in touch regarding Ruben. Stephanie was interested in the idea that they could put a stop to Ruben's treatment of women, but she was less convinced it was possible and fearful of how he might react.

And this was from the girl who had already put herself on the line to help.

It just showed the power that Ruben still held over her.

Olivia settled down in the office after saying a slightly embarrassed hello for her extra-long lunch break. If she wasn't careful she would be losing her job.

But she couldn't stop thinking about Ruben.

One problem that Stephanie had raised was that neither of them had a home address for Ruben. At least Stephanie had now provided her with Ruben's mobile number. But she had no desire to call him. And although seeing him face to face at the moment seemed equally unappealing, having a home address felt like it would help. There was no doubt that Ruben obviously wanted to keep his place of residence secret, and for that reason alone, it felt like a significant detail to obtain. Even though she had no idea what she was going to do if she got it.

She clicked open her emails, but while that was loading opened up a web page and searched for the site of the London School of Global Health.

Maybe they had contact details for him there.

There was a tab labelled 'Staff' and Olivia typed in the name Ruben Wilkins.

The search didn't come back with anything.

She thought back to what Stephanie had said. Ruben had told her the same story, that he was a PhD student, except it had been inspired by his experience in India, rather than Nepal. But Stephanie had poured cold water on the idea that it would be anywhere near the truth.

So she was probably wasting her time even looking at the institution.

However, Olivia didn't want to give up just yet. She began looking through the pages of each academic department, manually trawling through the staff lists. The lists were in alphabetical order, so it was actually quite a quick process.

There was no Ruben Wilkins.

'Hi, Olivia,' Henry said, causing her to actually jump in her seat with shock. In her deep thoughts about what to do with the Ruben situation, she hadn't noticed him approach. 'Looking to do a course?' he asked, talking over her shoulder as he stood dead straight directly behind her chair.

'Err, I...'

'I'm fully supportive of personal advancement,' he said, not really waiting for Olivia's attempt at an explanation. 'Life-long learning is the key to life-long living,' is my motto. Well, one of my mottos,' he laughed to himself. 'I mean, what is there left if not learning? We learn or we decay.'

Olivia clicked back on to her emails, willing to shut this conversation down. Henry could say some odd things at the best of times, and the girls in the office just put it down to him struggling valiantly to engage in meaningful conversation. But what he was coming out with now was particularly bizarre, even by his standards.

'I was just browsing,' Olivia managed, shifting her body ever-so-slightly away from Henry.

'London School of Global Health,' he said slowly and deliberately, 'I've heard very good things about it. Very good things. World leading. Good choice.'

'Like I said, I was just...'

'You're not thinking about leaving, are you?' he said, his expression darkening. 'I mean, I wouldn't like to think that you...'

'No, I'm not thinking of leaving...honestly.'

She smiled and he smiled back, reassured.

'That's good, wouldn't be the same here without you, Olivia.'

He moved back across to his desk and immediately set to work, headphones already sunk back into both ears. Olivia felt Katherine looking over at her, and she met her gaze briefly.

Giving herself a minute or so to let the office settle back down, she switched back to the internet and scrolled down to the bottom of the page, where she found the contact details for the university.

She scribbled down the number on a stray post-it note and, snatching up the note and her phone, retreated to the corridor. There was no way she was going to have this conversation in here.

~

'London School.'

Olivia leant against the window, watching the traffic crawl past on Euston Road below. Roadworks had sprung up overnight, reducing the lanes to one in each direction, causing a snarl up and horn-fest of buses and black cabs.

'Hi, can I speak to Ruben Wilkins please?' Olivia asked, as naturally as she could muster. 'He's a postgraduate researcher.'

'One moment, please.'

There were a few moments of silence, before Olivia got the response that she was expecting and had been predicted with such confidence by Stephanie.

'I'm afraid Ruben Wilkins isn't on our system.'

'So that means he doesn't study there?'

'All current employees and post-graduate research students are on the system,' she said.

'Well, thank you for checking...'

'He left employment at the School two months ago,' she cut in.

'Oh, right.'

So he *had* been there.

'I assume this is the same person you are looking for,' the call handler continued, sounding a little confused. 'But I don't have them down as a postgraduate student. They were a staff member, in the canteen. You did say Ruben Wilkins? W-i-l-k-i-n-s?'

'Yes, that should be him,' replied Olivia, excited that she

was actually getting somewhere. She hesitated, before deciding to dive right in. 'Is there a forwarding address?'

'There is, but I'm afraid I can't give out that information. I'm sorry, but I just can't.'

'Of course.'

'If you do want to get hold of him, then I suggest you could talk to his former colleagues down in the canteen. They're a friendly lot, I'm sure they'd be willing to help if they are able.'

That was actually a really good idea. 'Thank you, I think I'll do that.'

'You'll have to sign in as a guest to get access, but if you like I can take your name now in case one of my colleagues is on the front desk when you visit.'

'Thank you, it's Olivia Byron.'

'That's great, Olivia, I've got you down now, so there won't be a problem popping in to visit, if you decide to do so.'

'Thanks, I definitely will. You've been a great help.'

~

Unable to resist the temptation to follow up her lead, Olivia decided to take the rest of the afternoon off as time off in lieu and head to the university. The London School of Global Health was only a brisk few minutes' walk away.

She said a casual bye, earning no more than a cursory glance from the team. Katherine was too busy attacking an egg and cress sub-roll to enquire where she was going, Heather was on the phone to an outward bound centre in the Lake District, and Henry was fixed, very serious faced, on his screen.

Buoyed by the scent of success and progress, Olivia made

good time along the streets, and reached the university in under ten minutes.

She climbed the steps, and reported to reception, hoping that the lady she had spoken to would still be on duty.

It would just make it easier.

'Hi,' Olivia said, 'I called earlier, asking about someone who used to work here - Ruben Wilkins.'

'Ah, yes,' the lady replied, pulling her glasses from her forehead down onto her nose. 'It's Olivia Byron, yes?'

'Yes.'

The lady tapped a few keys, then turned around and grabbed a piece of paper from the printer behind her. 'Here you go,' she said, first folding and then slipping the paper into a plastic ID badge holder. 'If you can wear this at all times, that would be great.'

'Thanks,' Olivia said, looping it over her head.

'So,' the lady continued, 'the canteen is through those doors on the right, and then it's the first left, down the stairs.'

The canteen was surprisingly busy, and Olivia waited in the long line, wondering what the best way to approach this was.

She decided to be bold, skirting around the queue and heading straight for a member of staff who was collecting trays.

'Excuse me, I'm looking for Ruben Wilkins,' Olivia began. 'I think he used to work here.'

The woman glared at her.

'Used to work here,' she said, with a snort. 'Good riddance to bad rubbish.'

32

Cullen called through to the office and briefed Maggie Ferguson about events. He still needed to be very careful about his relationship with her, given his near-escape for subordination the previous week, and needed to play this by the book and operate under her authority.

Soon he would be freer, when the dust had settled, but not now.

'Thanks for letting me know, Paul,' she said, when he'd finished explaining as DI McGuire was also speaking to her boss about the same thing. 'Do you think this is an isolated incident, or should we be worried that this person will strike again?'

'I'm worried,' he admitted. 'But speaking to the family might reassure me.'

'Of course. You're about to do that?'

'We're on our way to her sister's flat now,' he explained. 'And Emily's parents have just come down from Edinburgh. My gut feeling is that they won't be particularly helpful, but the team are due to speak to them later. There are some work colleagues too, at the university, who we're planning to visit.'

'Sounds like a plan. You okay for resources?'

'I'm enlisting some of the Archangel team,' he explained, 'to look into whether this individual might already be on our radar. And we've also got the support from London division, even though we've got the lead now, of course.'

Given the gravity of the outcome, this case was now firmly under the jurisdiction of Cullen's National Serious and Organised Crime unit. But as usual, the regional force would provide support and co-operation as required.

'Good call. Well if there's anything you need, let me know. I appreciate that we might have something very significant on our hands here, and we want to make sure we give it the required attention.'

'Understood.'

Cullen then called straight through to DI Lomax, and briefed him in the same way. 'Let's get the team to go through any open cases relating to Archangel, look for similarities in modus operandi, physical appearance, anything that might spark something. Also, check with the local control centres, in case there have been any other incidents across the tube network that might have gone unreported to us. I'd also like someone to speak to Emily's parents, and we'll cover her colleagues at the university. We need to see if there's anything that points towards this being something other than a random event. Liaise with the London team, they're already working with us and will put time and effort into it, under our direction.'

'Yes, Boss.' He could sense Lomax wanting to ask the question. 'Who...who are you working with from the London team?' he asked finally, trying but failing to sound nonchalant.

'DI McGuire,' Cullen replied, actually looking over at Marianne, who had just come off the phone from her Chief Super.

'Oh,' he said instinctively, before checking himself. 'I mean, how is she?'

'She's good,' Cullen said, as Marianne approached, obviously intrigued by what was being said. 'Would you like to speak to her? I can put her on,' he added.

Marianne held up a hand and shook her head in protest, as Danny also declined. 'I'm okay, Boss.'

'Sorry,' Cullen said, to them both, already regretting his uncharacteristic moment of unprofessionalism. In truth, he said what he'd said out of genuine care for them both, but it wasn't his role to play matchmaker and he shouldn't have done it.

Fortunately both seemed to take it with good grace, judging by the mildly chastising smile from Marianne and the laugh from Lomax, unaccustomed to hearing Cullen feeling the need to apologise.

'C'mon,' Cullen said to Marianne as he cut the call. 'Let's get back down to business.'

EMILY'S SISTER, Karen Roberts, lived in Stratford, East London, in a new high rise apartment block overlooking the former site of the London 2012 Olympics. Over the past ten years, this part of the capital had been transformed from wasteland to an impressive cityscape, with the sprawling Westfield shopping centre, a series of high rise office blocks and hotels, and the various facilities that had played host to the world's greatest sporting competition.

Cullen and Marianne took the tube through to the end terminus of Stratford, skirting around the outskirts of the shopping centre and down past the stadium that once hosted international athletics but was now home to DS Beswick's beloved West Ham United Football Club.

'This place is impressive,' Marianne noted, as they crossed the street. 'But I don't know about you, it also makes me feel uneasy.'

Cullen thought that he knew what she meant. 'You mean the inequalities?'

'Yes. It's just so, in your face, d'you know what I mean?'

Cullen looked off to his left, to the other part of Stratford, across the busy main road that sliced its way between new and old, between shiny and dirty, between rich and poor. 'While people shop for Prada handbags, others are queuing outside food banks,' Cullen observed.

'It just all feels so wrong,' Marianne said. 'That there can be such disparities, such social injustice, and so obvious. But as a society we don't seem to be able to do anything about it, or don't want to do anything about it.'

'It's about power, and perceived value,' Cullen said. 'Those who hold the power have only a certain interest in changing the status quo. And only if they perceive there's value in it for them. Most of the welfare reforms over the past decades have been to try to respond to a problem for those already in power, not to help those in most need.'

Cullen had studied social policy at college, and as a police officer, was constantly reminded of how unequal systems and structures played out on the street.

'It's quite depressing,' Marianne replied. 'And we're left to fight the fires.'

'Extinguishing one blaze at a time,' Cullen agreed.

Cullen looked at his map app, on which he had keyed in the details of Karen Roberts' apartment block. 'Looks like it's that one, right in front,' he said.

'KAREN ROBERTS?' Cullen asked, as the attractive woman answered the apartment door. They'd been buzzed through downstairs and had travelled the ten floors by a lift that offered an impressive view across to the City of London.

Another reminder of the capital's contradictions.

'Yes,' she replied, unsmiling, a hand resting on the door as if for support. She looked very tired in the eyes, which was of course totally understandable.

'I'm Detective Chief Inspector Paul Cullen of the British Transport Police, from the National Serious and Organised Crime unit. This is my colleague, Detective Inspector Marianne McGuire, of the London division of the British Transport Police.

Marianne held out a hand, which Karen took with little enthusiasm.

'Do come in,' she said.

They followed her through to the living room, which also had a kitchen area off to the left. It was a pretty small place, as could be expected these days in London properties where space was premium.

'Would you like a drink?' Karen offered. She was wearing comfortable clothes that could have been pyjamas, her blonde hair tidied back tightly in a ponytail.

'We're okay,' Cullen replied, as Karen nodded and gestured for them to take a seat on the sofa opposite the chair where she sat down. 'Hopefully we won't keep you long,' he said, as they settled into position.

Karen shrugged, and looked like she was already battling back tears. 'It's okay, it's not like I have anything else to do. I'm signed off work. I'm just, you know, here, trying to get my head around...around it all.'

Her head dropped down to her knees, and Cullen nodded to Marianne, who was already looking at him with her unspoken suggestion.

Marianne moved across next to Karen and placed an arm around her back.

Cullen watched as Karen calmed almost immediately from the touch. Policing wasn't all about investigation and crime fighting. It was as much about care and compassion.

It was about the victims as much as the villains.

'We understand it's a lot to deal with,' Cullen said. 'It's been a terrible shock, I'm sure.'

Karen nodded, sniffing back tears as Marianne moved back slightly, but still within touching distance. 'I just can't believe she's gone.'

Cullen nodded. 'It will take time to process. I promise we won't be here a moment longer than is necessary.'

She nodded. 'It's okay, it's nice to have the company,' she sniffed. 'Sitting in this apartment by myself, it's not good really.'

'There are people who you can talk to,' Marianne responded.

She nodded. 'One of your colleagues let me know. I might call the number,' she said, referring to the victim of crime helpline.

'And if you don't want to talk to someone on that specific helpline, there are others of course.'

'Thank you.'

Cullen waited a few beats, watching Karen, just making sure she would be okay to start this. What they had to say would without doubt make things worse for the grieving sister, so they had to be very careful in how they approached it.

'We'd just like to ask you a few questions about your sister,' Cullen began. 'To help us get a fuller picture of her life.'

Karen's expression changed, as she began to realise that something wasn't as she'd expected. 'So,' she said slowly, processing her thoughts, 'you said you were with the serious crime unit?'

'The British Transport Police National Serious and Organised Crime unit,' Cullen reconfirmed, knowing just where this was going.

'But...serious crime...why would you...'

Be investigating an incident of someone accidentally or intentionally falling in front of train? Cullen heard in his head.

Good question, Karen.

This was the moment when everything would change for Karen Roberts. She had been grieving the suicide or accidental death of her sister, but at the end of his sentence she would enter a whole new world of mental trauma.

'We have reason to believe that Emily may have fallen onto the tracks while being pursued by someone,' Cullen revealed.

'What?' Karen said, stunned. 'Someone was following her?'

'That's our current assumption.'

He passed across his phone, with the image on screen showing the person in the baseball cap, standing on the platform shortly after Emily had fallen to her death.

'This person?' she said, her face twisted with confusion.

'Do they look familiar to you at all?' Marianne chipped in.

She shook her head, still looking at the individual.

'I'm afraid we don't have a better image,' Cullen added. 'Whoever it is was very deliberate in covering their face with the cap, so there are no shots of the person's face.'

'I still don't understand,' Karen replied. 'Someone did this to her? It wasn't an accident?'

'We believe she did fall, but there were contributing circumstances,' Cullen said. 'When did you last speak with Emily?'

'She texted me earlier that evening.'

They would check this on Emily's phone.

'And did she say anything unusual, anything that you might now think could be relevant to the investigation.'

'The investigation,' she mirrored, as if still coming to terms with the fact that her sister's death was no longer just a tragedy, it was a police investigation. 'No, it was normal, she just said maybe we could meet up at the weekend, go out for a meal down by the river.' Karen frowned at the memory of that last communication; such a mundane way to end things.

'So you didn't hear from her at all during her journey home?' Cullen pressed.

'No,' she said. 'But if she had been scared about something, then surely she would have called me.'

'Unless she couldn't,' Cullen said. Karen was probably right, Emily would have tried to call someone; if not her sister then someone else. 'She possibly didn't have a phone signal.'

'Right,' Karen noted, perturbed.

'Was Emily in a relationship?' Marianne asked.

Karen shook her head. 'Not for a few years.'

'No short term relationships?' Cullen added.

'No. Emily...it wasn't her focus. She was all about her career, she always said she didn't have time for a relationship. She was quiet and shy, too. Her last boyfriend was at university, and that was over ten years ago.'

'Emily was an academic?' Cullen asked.

'Yes, a Senior Research Fellow at the London School of Global Health. Emily was so dedicated to her career. It wasn't just a job, it was her life. Her expertise was on community-based interventions to reduce malaria infection. She was involved in a big trial in East Africa. She was supposed to be going out there soon...'

'I'm sorry,' Cullen said.

Karen shrugged. 'It's all gone now,' she stated flatly.

Cullen let that comment settle. 'Is it okay if I use your bathroom?' he asked.

'Yes, yes, of course.'

'Do you know anyone who Emily didn't get along with, anyone she might have mentioned, at work for example?' Cullen continued, as he returned from the bathroom.

'No,' she replied confidently. 'Emily got on really well with her colleagues. She'd been there for years, and said one of the reasons why she'd stayed is because of the people she worked with. I never heard her say a bad word about any colleagues.'

'Good,' Cullen said, not really thinking that at all. He'd thought the workplace would be one of the most likely sources of Emily's pursuer, but it wasn't looking that way.

At least not on the surface.

'Can I ask a personal question?' Cullen said.

'Of course,' she replied. 'Anything to help.'

'Did you trust your sister?'

The question seemed to surprise her. 'Trust Emily? Yes, of course I trusted her.' She straightened herself in the seat. 'I don't understand. Why would you ask that?'

'So you don't think she may have kept anything significant in her life from you?' he continued, ignoring her somewhat defensive response.

'Nothing significant,' she replied. 'I mean, everyone has secrets. But we were close - so no, I don't think she kept anything important from me.'

Cullen nodded along, watching to see if she would reveal anything non-verbally during her rebuttal.

'It's just that if the person was known to Emily, then it's highly likely that you know them too, and they know you.'

Again he looked for a reaction, before continuing.

'So if anyone does come to mind, please do let us know right away.'

'I will,' she replied. 'I'll do that, of course I will.'

'Much appreciated.' Then came the slightly unfair curveball. 'Are you in a relationship at the moment?'

'No,' came back the instant reply. 'I'm single too.'

He watched Karen for a second or two, as she held his gaze before looking away.

Cullen exchanged a serious look with Marianne. 'I think that's it for now,' he said, turning his attention back to Karen Roberts. 'Unless there's anything else you would like to ask, or think might be useful for us to know?'

'No, but if I think of anything I'll let you know.'

'Thank you. And once again, we're really very sorry about your loss.'

33

Karen Roberts watched the detectives as they walked away from the apartment block. Her eyes traced their path down the street, but her mind drifted onto other things.

Poor Emily.

She wrapped her arms tightly around her waist, trying to comfort herself against the feelings that threatened to rise up like an incoming tide and consume her.

She shook herself back into the here and now, focussing again on the two detectives.

My God, they're looking up at me!

They were. Both of them. But the man in particular, Cullen, he seemed to have her directly in his sights, as if offering her a personal message, or maybe challenge, across the distance.

Could he see her?

There were times in the interview that she thought he could read her thoughts, and see through the lies. The way he had looked at her, it had set her on edge.

She shuddered again, jumping at the sound of a door slamming shut in the apartment upstairs.

Suddenly she needed *him* here again. She didn't want to be alone, with only memories and regrets for company. She broke away from the window and fetched the phone.

'Please pick up, please pick up...'

'Hi.'

'I need you to come over,' she said, her breath ragged.

'Again? Already?' the amused voice replied. 'I obviously didn't do my job properly earlier.'

'Oh no, you did, you *really* did,' she replied, forgetting herself.

'So well you can't wait for more?' he teased.

'The police were here,' she said.

There was a pregnant pause. 'Asking about Emily?'

'Yes.'

'And?'

'They think someone else was involved in her death.'

He actually laughed at that. 'Well, of course someone else was involved.'

34

'What do you think?' Cullen asked, as they exited the building and started their walk back to the station.

'I'm not sure,' Marianne said.

Cullen turned, amused. 'Not sure about what?'

'Not sure about Karen Roberts,' she replied, as they continued their walk. 'I didn't think there was anything untoward until the last few minutes. Seemed like the usual grieving relative. But at the end. Well, I'm not so sure. How about you?'

'I'm not sure either,' Cullen replied, with a wry smile. He stopped and looked back at the tower block, setting his sights on the tenth floor.

Was that someone watching from one of the windows?

'When you asked her if she trusted Emily, there was something about her reaction, something I can't quite put my finger on,' Marianne noted. 'Is she watching us?' she asked suddenly, shoulder to shoulder with Cullen.

'Possibly.' It wasn't very easy to see for certain, with the sun reflecting off the glass, but there definitely could have been a figure there. And even if she had been standing there, it didn't mean anything. He turned back around. 'I thought she looked scared,' he said at last.

'Scared?' Marianne said, also having turned away from the building. 'Of what?'

'That's what I'm not sure about.'

'Why did you ask whether she was in a relationship?'

'Why do you think?'

'Because if she is, they might be the person of interest?'

'That's true,' he said. 'But it's not the reason.'

Marianne shrugged. 'Go on...'

'Because I wanted to see what she looks like when she's lying.'

'You think she was lying about being in a relationship?'

'Definitely.'

'How can you be so sure?'

'A few clues in the flat,' he said.

She looked surprised and a little disappointed that she might have missed something significant. 'Really?'

'The dishes by the sink,' he replied. 'Another person had been there for breakfast.'

'You think?'

'I think.'

'Might have been a friend. Or family?'

'I very much doubt it.'

'How can you be so sure?'

'Because I found a used condom in the bathroom bin.'

'Do you think it's significant that she lied?' Marianne asked, as they entered Stratford tube station, passing through the ticket barriers and heading towards the westbound platform.

'Maybe,' Cullen said, noting from the electronic display that the next tube train was due to depart in one minute. 'Fancy a run?'

Marianne accepted the challenge and they sprinted off towards the train, skimming in through the doors just as the departure beep sounded and the train set off.

'You move fast for an older guy,' Marianne joked, as they both regained their breath.

'Thanks,' Cullen deadpanned, doing what he always did now when entering a tube carriage - looking around to see if there was anyone on board who might be a possible sex offender.

Operation Archangel had ruined his tube train experience, good and proper. Carriages were no longer just a means of transportation; they were potential crime scenes where the vulnerable were preyed upon.

It was a cynical lens from which to look through life, but a natural consequence of being immersed in the reality of what exactly went on under the streets of London.

That wasn't to overstate the threat. For the millions of people using the tube system every day, they would never come to any harm, never feel fear. But some definitely would, and they were the ones to whom Cullen and his colleagues owed their time and effort.

'You okay?' Marianne asked.

Cullen was looking down the carriage, and through the doors to the next compartment.

He was looking at the person with their back to them, holding on to a pole, wearing a baseball cap.

'I'm fine,' Cullen answered, only half with her. The person turned and Cullen got a full sight of their face. It was a black guy, in their late teens or early twenties.

He looked away. There was no point scrutinising every person on the tube who was wearing a baseball cap.

THE TUBE WASN'T a place to discuss sensitive business, so Cullen and Marianne waited until they'd arrived at their destination before picking up the conversation again.

They alighted at Euston Square, a tube station right at the top of Euston Road, not more than a hundred metres or so from where Cullen had chased the man the previous week.

Cullen knew that Marianne would be aware of what had happened - the story had been extremely high profile and the talk of the force - but she hadn't mentioned it and he was grateful for her restraint.

The events were still playing on his mind.

The man crushed, dying underneath the wheels of the lorry...

And the girlfriend, understandably horrified by the sight that met her.

You've murdered my boyfriend!

He shook off the unwelcome memories that clung on to him like gargoyles.

'So, what do we think about Karen Roberts now?' he said, as they headed down Euston Road, en route to their destination of the London School of Global Health.

'More question marks, definitely, after what you told me. You think she knows more about what happened to Emily?'

'Not necessarily. But she did lie about the relationship thing.'

'Maybe it was a one night stand,' Marianne suggested, as they waited to cross a side street. 'And she didn't class that as being in a relationship.'

'Possibly.'

'Is there anything else that makes you suspicious?'

'The way she looked when I asked about trust.'

'About whether she trusted Emily?'

Cullen nodded. 'Her answer wasn't convincing.'

'Which is why you took the opportunity to check out her bathroom?' She smiled.

'I did actually need to go,' he admitted. 'But, yes.'

'So if we go with the line that she is in a relationship, but doesn't want us to know, the question is why?'

'Any ideas?' Cullen batted back.

'Maybe she's having an affair. Maybe she wants to keep it secret to protect him.'

'Definitely possible,' Cullen agreed.

'Or maybe she's ashamed.'

'Go on...'

'Maybe she's ashamed for some reason, I don't know, maybe again because the person is married, or maybe some other reason...'

'Again, possible.'

'I guess the question is, is it relevant to the case? If it's not, then we don't need to think too much about it, do we?'

'We have to assume it is relevant,' Cullen replied, as they neared the corner where the university was located. 'Even if it isn't.'

'Of course.'

'It's like I said. If this person was known to Emily, then it's highly likely that they are also known to Karen.'

'And vice versa.'

'Exactly.'

'So we'll definitely be paying Karen Roberts another visit.'

35

Olivia exited Notting Hill Gate tube station, still wondering whether her plan, if you could call it a plan, was possibly the most ridiculous thing she had ever considered.

She'd called Stephanie to let her know that she now had Ruben's home address, given to her freely by the lady behind the university canteen, and had expected her to jump at the chance of confronting him. But instead, Stephanie, feeling it was too dangerous, had warned her in no uncertain terms not to take action.

And yet, here she was, just under a mile from Ruben's flat, intent on facing him and extracting some kind of truth.

But why?

It was a question she had asked herself over and over again on the journey here. But even though a clear answer hadn't emerged, the overwhelming urge to do this had intensified rather than diminished.

So she was going to do this.

She would walk right up to his door.

And confront him.

Tell him that she knew the truth.

Tell him that he needed to stop what he was doing.

She referred to her maps app, crossing the street at the lights and turning left along the high street, past Costa Coffee and a myriad of interesting coffee shops, delicatessens, grocers and a bakery.

She turned off the high street, down a long straight road that was flanked by pleasant Victorian townhouses.

Ruben certainly lived in a nice part of London.

How could he afford this, working serving coffee?

Olivia consulted the phone again. She was right there. Looking across the street, she saw the property. It was another lovely house, presumably split into two flats.

Taking a deep, steadying breath, she crossed the street.

She felt there was no going back now.

Shaking with nerves, Olivia buzzed through to Ruben's flat. When there was no response after three buzzes, she felt a strange mixture of relief and disappointment.

She turned to walk away.

'Hello?'

Turning back, she knew this was it. 'It's Olivia,' she said, into the microphone.

There was silence for a few seconds before the door clicked open.

'You'd better come in. Straight up the stairs.'

~

Olivia entered. There was a door to the left, for the ground floor flat, and the staircase ahead of her up to Ruben's first floor dwelling. He was standing at the top door, waiting for her as she reached the top of the stairs.

'You're an unexpected visitor,' he smiled, appearing genuinely pleased to see her. 'Please, do come in.'

She followed him through into the flat, which was furnished just as Olivia would have expected. There was an electric guitar hanging from the white painted wall, flanked by stylish black and white images of New Zealand landscapes. The furniture was straight out of a style magazine, black leather sofa and glass coffee table, with a retro record player in the corner alongside a stack of vinyl discs, and across from that a large Apple Mac computer monitor.

'Would you like a coffee?' he said breezily, seemingly at ease with the sudden appearance of Olivia at his home.

'A glass of water would be great,' Olivia said, continuing to look around the place, yet not wanting to seem nosey.

'No problem,' he replied. 'Please, do take a seat.'

She did as directed, sinking down into the soft leather, hearing Ruben fill the glass from the next door kitchen. She wondered how the hell she was going to play this, and what Ruben was really thinking.

'Here you go,' he said, still bright and light. He took a seat in the single chair opposite. 'So,' he smiled, a little too widely Olivia couldn't help but think, 'How are you?'

'I'm good,' she said. 'Good.'

'Great,' he replied, clasping his hands as if in prayer. 'So, do you like the place?'

'It's lovely,' Olivia replied, honestly. 'Really nice.'

'Good, good, glad you like it.' He smiled again but it faded as he continued to stare at her. It was as if he was looking through her, and his altered expression was unsettling. 'So,' he said, shaking himself back into focus, smiling once again, but this time with obvious strain, 'how did you know where I live?'

Olivia had prepared for this question. 'Clive gave me your address,' she said, referring to his colleague at the café. She didn't want to admit the extent to which she'd been snooping on Ruben, and his past.

'No,' he said simply. 'No, he didn't.'

Olivia was taken aback by the certainty of Ruben's tone. But she felt she had no choice but to press on with the lie, fearing what might happen if the truth came out. 'He did, honestly.'

Ruben shook his head. 'He didn't, Olivia.'

'Honestly.'

'Stop lying to me,' Ruben replied calmly. 'Just tell me the truth. I know you're lying, because Clive doesn't have this address. I used another one.'

Another one?

'So, just tell me the truth, Olivia.'

'Someone you used to work with at the university gave it to me,' she admitted.

He nodded, satisfied. 'I thought so.'

Olivia waited for Ruben to say more, and when he didn't her discomfort increased.

'I just wanted to see you,' she said, filling the gaping void.

He nodded. 'Well like I said, it's good to see you.'

Except now he didn't look like he meant it.

Olivia had a sudden desire to just get up and leave, end it all here, walk away and get on with her life. But the words were already leaving her mouth. 'Why did you lie?'

He seemed surprised by the question, cocking his head. 'Lie?'

'You lied about...everything.'

He laughed. 'Wow,' he said, 'wow!' he repeated, blinking away mocked disbelief. 'I lied about *everything*?'

'Yes. You lied about what happened in Australia. The car crash, your friends dying, it was all made up. You weren't in a band. You lied about going to Nepal. You lied about doing a doctorate.'

Ruben put up a finger. 'You probably should watch what you're saying,' he warned.

But now Olivia had started, she felt galvanised and empowered. She was speaking on behalf of all the girls who had been badly treated by this man. 'You cheat on women. You treat people terribly. Why do you do it, Ruben?'

'You want to know why I do it?' he said. 'Because I can.'

'Because you can?' She felt like she was listening to a warped doppelganger of the man with whom she had shared a bed, a man who she had thought might actually be The One.

'Yes, because I can. I like women, and they like me,' he replied. 'To be honest, I don't exactly need to try hard to attract women. Do I, Olivia?'

Olivia found herself shaking her head.

'Is that a problem?' he asked, amused by her reaction.

'Ask your victims,' she said.

Again, he looked amused, and leant forward in his seat. '*Victims*?'

'Stephanie told me what you did to her,' Emily replied. 'The gaslighting. Her cat.'

'Lies,' he said. 'The cat ran away. I tried to find it. She's bitter because our relationship ended; that's all.'

'I don't think so. Why did you lie to me about who she was?'

'Because she was trying to make trouble between us.'

'She was making trouble for you,' Olivia corrected.

He didn't dispute that. 'What did you come here for,

Olivia? To warn me off from my wicked ways? To convince me to turn over a new leaf, settle down as a family man with two kids and a wife? Maybe even a cat?'

'I don't know why I came,' she admitted.

This seemed to embolden him, and Olivia quickly realised that her response had been a mistake, with Ruben taking her lack of purpose as an admission of weakness. He smiled. 'What *exactly* did Stephanie say I did?'

'You tried to control her life.'

'Really?'

'And did you ever feel that I was trying to control you, Olivia?'

'No. But...'

'I think you should go now,' he said, 'while we're still on relatively good terms. Unless of course, you would like to take this into the bedroom?'

His expression was chilling.

Olivia stood.

She needed to get out of here. Now.

'Come on, Olivia, let's kiss and make up, shall we? I remember how much you enjoyed the experience last night.'

'I need to go now,' she said, forcing herself to look him in the eye as he stood between her and the door.

At last he nodded. 'Suit yourself,' he said, standing aside and gesturing theatrically towards the door. 'I have plenty of options,' he added. 'Plenty *better* options.'

Olivia reached the door, imagining that he might grab her from behind as the warning from Stephanie came to mind.

You're in danger.

But he let her go, out into the small hallway and down the steep stairs. She was breathless by the time she reached the outer door, her imagination still in overdrive.

He'll cut you off before you can get outside.

She fumbled with the door.

You'll be his prisoner and no-one else knows you're here.

It wouldn't open.

'Shit,' she said under her breath. She pulled it again. 'Shit.'

'Having trouble?' he mocked from the top of the staircase.

Olivia ignored his jibe and continued her efforts to escape.

'Push the door away from you first, then pull back,' he said.

She did just that, and the door came open, letting in welcome fresh air and the chance for freedom.

She hurried through the gap and down the path, out onto the pavement, not looking back to see if he was following.

'Love you, Olivia!' she heard him shout. 'It was great! Until next time!'

36

Cullen and Marianne looked up at the impressive building that housed the London School of Global Health. It was one of the world's leading schools for public health, with a particular strength in tackling global infectious disease. They had been at the forefront of the advances against malaria in sub-Saharan Africa, and had played a vital role in the response to the SARS crisis back in 2002.

'Been here before?' Marianne asked.

'No. You?'

'My cousin studied here,' she revealed. 'She works in public health, in Bristol. Did her masters here a few years ago. I attended her graduation in this building.'

They climbed the white stone steps and reported to reception. A few minutes later a balding, jovial man passed through the security doors and approached them.

'Detectives?' he asked.

Cullen nodded. 'Detective Chief Inspector Paul Cullen, and Detective Inspector Marianne McGuire of the British Transport Police. And you're Professor Hoffman?' he asked in return, as he shook the man's hand. Professor Hoffman was Emily's line manager, and head of the Department of Infectious Diseases.

'That's me,' he said, as they released the handshake and Hoffman also greeted Marianne.

'Thank you for agreeing to see us,' Cullen said. 'I know you must be busy.'

Professor Hoffman waved the thought away. 'Oh, no, please, no need for thanks. We were all devastated, are *still* devastated at the news about poor Emily. Anything we can do to help, *anything*, then we will do it. Without question. The work, frankly, though important of course, can wait.'

Cullen nodded, while thinking that this guy seemed to be a perfect embodiment of what he imagined a nutty professor to be like. His manner, his attire - tweed jacket with patches on his elbows, red trousers - and his white hair, sticking out at angles, that looked messy and unkempt but could have actually been a style that was cultivated to fit his role.

'That's good to hear,' Cullen said. 'Is there somewhere we can go to talk in private?'

'Of course. I've commandeered the staff room, to give us a bit of space to play around in.'

Cullen felt it was an odd choice of words, but nodded and they followed him through the doors and along the wood-panelled corridors.

'Here we go,' the Professor said, as they entered the staff room. 'Our little island of rest and repose in a sea of turbulence. Please, do take a seat. Can I get either of you a drink?' he said, gesturing over to the kitchen area.

'I'm okay,' Cullen replied. 'Thank you.' Marianne also politely refused.

'Let's get down to it then,' the Professor replied, clasping his hands together.

'So,' Marianne began, taking up the lead for this interview. 'As we explained on the phone, we'd like to find out some more about Emily and her life at the university.'

'Of course, of course,' he said, looking at Cullen. 'I mean, I understand that if someone takes their own life, it's only reasonable, sensible, to explore what might have pushed them to do something so drastic. And I appreciate that for many, the workplace could be a factor, maybe *the* factor, in explaining what happened. But I just want to take the opportunity to assure you how happy Emily is, was, at work. She just adored what she did, she really...'

'That's good to know,' Marianne interrupted, to the Professor's obvious surprise. 'And although we haven't ruled out suicide, that is only one line of enquiry.'

'Oh?' he said, shocked. You could see his brain whirring. 'Oh. I don't, you see, I thought...'

The Professor looked over at Cullen again for explanation, but Cullen resisted the temptation to respond. This was Marianne's.

'Who did Emily work with predominantly?' she asked.

He actually recoiled at this question. 'Well, me of course,' he said. 'The projects that Emily worked on were all under my leadership as the PI.'

'PI?'

'Sorry, Primary Investigator,' he explained.

'And who else?' she pressed.

'Well, we have a fairly tightly knit team,' he explained. 'I lead the group, and underneath there are two senior research fellows, three research fellows, including Emily, and then two junior researchers. We also have doctoral students.'

'And how are relationships within the team?' Marianne enquired.

'Superb,' he replied, without hesitation. 'We're like a family.'

'Families can sometimes fall out,' she tested.

The Professor smiled. 'Indeed. And yes, there are tensions from time to time. But believe me, detectives, it is a very happy working environment, which I pride myself on. You can ask any of my team, and I'm sure they will attest to that fact.'

'We will,' Marianne said.

'A happy team is a productive team,' the Professor stated. 'And a productive team is a successful team.'

'Indeed,' Marianne replied, evidently not quite knowing how to respond to that comment.

'So detectives,' the Professor said. 'I must admit, I'm confused about what exactly you're looking for here. I want to be able to be as helpful as possible, you see.'

He looked again at Cullen, seemingly longing for the intervention of the male, senior detective. But still, Cullen wasn't going to bite.

Why should he?

Marianne glanced across at Cullen and he nodded, understanding the unspoken request. They were already working well together, and Cullen felt a flash of guilt at that thought when he remembered that his actual partner was at that moment lying in a hospital bed after a near-death experience.

'Do you know anyone that might wish to cause Emily harm?' Marianne asked.

Again he visibly recoiled. 'Harm Emily? No, no, of course not, most definitely not.'

'She didn't say anything to you about being fearful of anyone? No instances of her being followed?'

'No, absolutely not.' He thought some more. 'You think someone killed her?'

'Emily fell onto the tracks,' Marianne confirmed. 'But we have reason to believe that she was being followed shortly before the event.'

'Oh. And you think it could be one of my team?'

'We can't rule anything out at this stage.'

'No, of course not, of course you can't. And you shouldn't,' he said, thinking to himself, 'you need to keep an open mind, free from bias, and from the mists of doubt, truth will emerge.'

'I wish it was always that easy,' Cullen couldn't help but comment.

The Professor fixed him with a stare and straightened in his seat. 'Detective, I know my team well, as I said, they are like family. I don't for one moment think that any one of them are capable of something like this. However, in the spirit of transparent and rigorous investigation, I will do all in my power to assist you.'

'Thank you,' Cullen replied, appreciating the co-operation but thinking uncharitably that they would do whatever it took anyway to get to the truth, with or without the Professor's assistance.

THE PROFESSOR WAS true to his word, and had already readied the research team to be available for questioning.

Again Marianne led the discussions, which they held

one-on-one in the staff room. Of the team, two of the six were male, and they left those to the end.

'So, what do you think?' Cullen asked Marianne, as the last of the four female co-workers left the staff room after being gently but rigorously quizzed.

'I think I wish I worked here,' she joked. 'I mean, I didn't even know people could be so happy and content at work.'

'Me neither. We're obviously in the wrong job,' Cullen replied.

'I mean, apart from the fact that they were all understandably shocked by what's happened, they all just seemed so happy. No sign of disharmony. Just like the Professor said.'

'Just like the Professor said,' Cullen echoed.

'You think he coached them on what to say?' Marianne said, picking up on her partner's insinuation.

'Well it was a bit like they were reading from a script,' Cullen said. 'I think I heard the words "one big family" and "close-knit team" from each of them.'

'Yes, you did. But they seemed genuine.'

'Yes, they did.'

'And no hint of anything going on in Emily's life that might explain what happened.'

'No. Absolutely nothing,' he agreed. 'I think this is probably a dead end, but let's take the two guys and see what they've got to say.'

THE FIRST MAN'S account tallied perfectly with those of the women before him. And once again, the script was remarkably consistent. Emily was a happy, dedicated researcher who was a popular, established team member. The Senior Research Fellow, Peter Carter, couldn't offer anything that suggested any threat to Emily emanating from the workplace environment.

Then came the final staff member.

'Hello,' the man said, taking the seat opposite. He introduced himself as Nasrul Ahmed, a junior researcher from Malaysia who had worked closely with Emily on the malaria project in East Africa. He looked nervous and upset.

'Emily was such a good person,' he began, his hands on his knees like a schoolboy posing for a photo. 'She helped me so much, so kind to me when I arrived here last year. I can't believe she's gone. It just doesn't feel real.'

Marianne and Cullen replied with words of consolation, before Marianne explained the context behind the investigation while he listened intently.

'Was Emily happy?' Marianne asked, after she had finished the explanation.

'Until recently,' was his surprising reply.

'Oh?' Marianne said, her interest piqued by this minority report - no-one else had so much as hinted at anything but a positive picture of her life.

'Ever since I met Emily, she was a very happy person,' he explained. 'She loved her job, and it was, you know, infectious. It made me want to do better, you know, for the project that we were working on. But a few months ago, I noticed a change.'

'A change?'

'She seemed different somehow,' he said. 'Not quite herself.'

'In what way?'

He shrugged. 'Just less happy. Less herself.'

'Did you ask her what the matter was?'

'Yes,' he said. 'I did ask her, one day, we were in the canteen, and she just seemed so, so miserable, you know? All of a sudden. It was like a dark cloud had just enveloped her. I asked her what the matter was.'

'And what did she say?'

'She said she'd been having relationship problems.'

'Did she say with who?'

'No. She didn't want to talk about it, I could tell. I didn't know she was even in a relationship, but I wasn't surprised really that she hadn't mentioned anything before - even though she was a very friendly person, she was also quiet and private - like a lot of people in academia.'

'And you really have no idea who she might have been having these relationship problems with?' Cullen interjected. 'It could be very significant, so please, think hard.'

Nasrul puffed his cheeks as he thought, then exhaled. 'I'm sorry, I really don't know. Sorry.'

'It's okay,' Cullen replied, watching as the guy actually was blushing at his inability to help. 'But if anything does come to you, then please do get in touch.'

'I will,' he promised, 'I definitely will. I want to help you to find out what happened to my friend. It just won't be the same without her around here.'

Cullen and Marianne both nodded.

'I promise, Nasrul,' Cullen said, 'we're going to do all in our power to uncover the truth.'

'I just can't imagine that anyone would want to do any harm to Emily,' he said. 'She was such a lovely, wonderful person. What kind of individual would want to hurt her?'

'That's what we intend to find out,' Marianne replied.

Nasrul nodded. 'I'll have more of a think,' he said. 'Something may come to me.'

37

He watched from behind the white tradesman's van, which was parked across the street, as Olivia emerged from the property opposite.

She was flustered, hurrying, like she didn't want people to see her.

But *he* had seen her.

Just like he had seen her enter the university.

He traced her path out onto the pavement as she turned right, the direction from where she had arrived, and walked off at pace.

About to set off in pursuit, he froze in horror at the sight of the man emerging from the property.

His worst fears had been realised.

It was him.

The man from the café.

'Love you, Olivia!' the good-looking man shouted adoringly. He was half-dressed, his hairy, muscled chest on display for all to see, his jeans slung low around his slim waist. 'It was great! Until next time!'

It was great?

Until next time?

He seethed and boiled with anger and jealousy, but stayed stock-still until the man, the one that Olivia had been lusting over recently so pathetically, retreated inside.

It was great...

His body was fizzing, his fists curled into tight white balls of fury.

Olivia was still in sight, some way down the road, and he now knew what he had to do.

Maybe it was always meant to be this way.

Like Romeo and Juliet.

38

'I hope you found your visit helpful?' the Professor said, as he re-entered the room following Nasrul's exit.

'Yes, thank you,' Cullen said, moving to stand. 'Thank you for your co-operation.'

'Absolutely no problem, Detective,' he replied. 'I trust my team provided a good insight into the way things are here?'

'Indeed they did,' Cullen replied, not appreciating the fishing expedition that the Professor had embarked on. 'It's all confidential, of course,' he couldn't help but add.

'Confidential, of course, Detective, of course.'

'Glad you understand. Thanks again for your help.'

'My pleasure,' the Professor said. 'And if there is anything you need, then please don't hesitate to get in touch.'

'We will,' Cullen said. 'Can you direct us to the canteen?'

'Why, yes, of course,' he said. 'I'm afraid I've got a meeting now, so I can't stay, but I can certainly take you there and you'll be able to find your own way out, I'm sure.'

'That would be great, thanks.'

The Professor left them at the canteen entrance, and

Cullen breathed a sigh of relief that they were free to discuss things without him.

The canteen was quiet, with just a smattering of people spread across the quite large underground room.

The grabbed a couple of coffees and settled down in the corner.

'I didn't take to that guy,' Marianne admitted.

'Who, the Professor?'

'Yes.'

'Me neither, but I don't think he's our suspect.'

Marianne laughed. 'Nor me.'

'Although we shouldn't rule anyone out,' Cullen said, with all seriousness.

'Even Nasrul?'

'Even Nasrul.'

Just then Cullen's phone rang.

It was DI Lomax.

'Just updating you Boss,' he said, sparing the niceties. 'We've just come back from talking with Emily's parents.'

'Yes...'

'Poor people are in pieces,' he said. 'But they were actually more helpful than I thought they might be. They said that Emily called them a few weeks ago, upset, saying that she'd had enough of London and was thinking of moving back up to Edinburgh.'

Cullen looked at DI McGuire, who was trying to listen in. 'Did they say why?'

'Emily wouldn't tell them details, but had mentioned about something to do with someone at work.'

'A relationship?'

'That's what they assumed, but like I said, she didn't want to go into details.'

Cullen thought back to what Karen Roberts had said about Emily not having been in a relationship for a number of years.

Of course, it didn't mean she was lying.

Emily could have kept a relationship secret.

But was that likely?

And why would she lie about it?

'Did they say anything else?'

'Yes. It seems that the situation for Emily improved. Just this week she called, saying that she'd decided to stay in London after all, and that the problem had gone away.'

'The problem had gone away,' Cullen repeated, thinking through what that probably meant. He could now see a way forward, and just hoped that it wouldn't be a false trail. 'Is there anything else of note that her parents said?'

'No, Boss, that was it. I did feel so sorry for them, like I said, they are really in bits about it.'

'We're doing our best for them,' Cullen reassured. 'But I know that whatever we do, won't be enough.'

'No.'

'Any word yet back from the control teams?'

'Not yet,' DI Lomax replied. 'I'm hoping to hear something in the next hour or so, and if I don't I'll chase.'

'Good, thanks. You never know, something might turn up, somewhere on the network.'

'Although I'm worried about the false positives,' Lomax raised, referring to the cases that might emerge that could have nothing to do with their suspect and may result in wasted time and effort.

'We need to be fairly rapid at sorting the wheat from the chaff,' Cullen agreed. 'We know what we're looking for, and there are enough people on the case. I'm hoping they'll do the filtering before sending anything through.'

'It should be fine,' DI Lomax concurred. 'Although I think it's a long shot that it will lead to a breakthrough.'

'Me too, but it's more than worth checking. Let me know when you hear back.'

'Agreed. Will do, Boss.'

Cullen turned to DI McGuire. 'Did you catch any of that?'

'Only from what you said. There hasn't been anything yet from the control rooms. And there's something Emily's parents said about her being in a relationship.'

'A relationship here,' Cullen expanded.

'Oh, right,' she said. 'Now that *is* interesting.'

'Yes, it is. They said she was so upset about something that she was planning to quit London, and move back up to Edinburgh.'

'When was this?'

'A few weeks ago.'

'But she stayed...'

'They said she changed her mind this week, and that the problem had gone away.'

'The *person* had gone away,' Marianne said, on the same wavelength as her senior colleague.

'My thoughts exactly.'

'So we go back to her colleagues, see if they can shed any more light on the situation?'

'Not yet,' Cullen replied. 'First of all, we need to have a conversation with human resources. I want the details of every employee and student who has left this place over the past three months.'

The list of those who had left the institution in the past three months was mercifully short.

'Just ten people,' Cullen noted, as they sat back in their original seats down in the canteen.

Marianne looked across at the sheet which the office worker had helpfully provided them with, following their request just twenty minutes earlier.

'And only four men,' Cullen added.

'There's nothing to say it couldn't be a woman,' Marianne corrected, with a smile.

'True,' he said. 'Very true.'

He looked down the list. The employee had helpfully included the person's job description alongside their name and date when they ceased employment at the university.

'This guy here,' Cullen said. 'He worked down here, in the canteen.'

'Ruben Wilkins,' Marianne said. She looked across towards the serving counter, where three staff members were chatting, taking advantage of the absence of customers. She looked back at Cullen. 'Strike while the iron's hot?'

'I was planning to go back to Nasrul with the list as a first step, but yes, why not?'

'Hi, we were wondering if we could have a brief chat, about one of your ex-colleagues,' Cullen said, cutting into the workers' conversation.

The three stopped their chatter dead, with looks that surprised both Cullen and Marianne.

'Detective Chief Inspector Paul Cullen of the British Transport Police,' Cullen said, showing them his ID.

'And Detective Inspector Marianne McGuire,' Marianne added, also revealing her identification.

The workers looked at one another, as if deciding on a course of action.

'About Ruben Wilkins?' one of them said, a middle aged lady with soft features.

'Yes, that's right,' Cullen replied, intrigued as to how they had immediately honed in on the correct person.

'You know, you're the second person to ask about him today.'

'Oh?' Cullen said, now very interested. 'Is there somewhere we can go to discuss things, in private?'

'In the back,' the lady said. 'We can go in the back. Pete, Mike, you're okay to man the front?' she asked the two men who were with her.

They agreed and Cullen and Marianne were invited around the side of the serving area and into a back room that acted as their staff room.

'It's a bit tight, but if you both breathe in we should be alright,' the lady said, pulling in an extra chair from outside.

They all squashed around the small white table.

'So, you want to know about Ruben Wilkins?' she said, her face stern. 'My name's Angie, by the way.'

'Please,' Cullen said. 'And nice to meet you, Angie.'

'What has he done?' she asked, looking at the two officers in turn.

'Possibly nothing,' Cullen replied, far too experienced to risk prejudicing any evidence that they might be about to receive. 'So, Ruben Wilkins worked with you?'

'Yes,' she replied. 'He wasn't here long, just six months, but he was a popular member of the team, at first.'

'At first?'

'Until I found out what he had been doing.'

'Which was?'

'Cheating on my niece, Carly.'

'And your niece, she works here?'

'Yes. She's not here today. It's her day off. But usually she works behind the counter, with us.'

'So your niece was in a relationship with Ruben Wilkins?'

'Yes. For a few months. I didn't know about it at first, but when I found out, I was happy.' She laughed bitterly. 'I was under the impression that he was a nice guy, the kind of guy who you would want to be in your family. But it turns out I was wrong.'

'Your niece discovered that he was cheating on her?'

She nodded, barely able to control her anger, even after this time. 'He really hurt her. Carly's a lovely girl. But the cheating, that wasn't the worst part, that's not what upset me the most. It was his reaction that really got to me.'

'And that was?'

'Like he just didn't care.'

'That's what Carly told you?'

She shook her head. 'When she found out, she had to take a few days off, the poor love, she was so upset - she just couldn't face him. But *I* could.'

Marianne leant forward. 'So what did Ruben say, exactly?'

'I can remember the exact words,' she replied. 'Because he didn't say much. I must admit, I launched a bit of a tirade against him - it was in this very room. I was so angry. I mean, I can get angry, I really can, when there's good reason. And people know it. People know not to wind me up. But this guy,' she snorted, 'this guy, he just sat there, soaking it all up like a sponge, with a smile on his lips; can you believe it? I mean, it made me even more mad. And then finally I'd said all I needed to say, and you know what he said?'

Cullen and Marianne shook their heads in unison, giving her the cue to continue.

She smiled disbelievingly at the recollection and shook her head. 'He said: "Is that everything?" And then he got up, grabbed his bag, and left. That was the last we saw of him. No explanation. No apology. Not to me or to my Carly.'

'So he quit there and then,' Cullen sought to confirm.

'Yes,' she said. 'At least he did the one decent thing. Not that he'd have had a choice. If he'd have so much as set foot in this place again, I would have been after him.'

The anger was still burning, clear to see.

'The person who Ruben was having a relationship with,' Cullen asked. 'Do you know who it is?'

'Yes, I do,' she replied. 'Her name is Emily. And she's a researcher here.'

Cullen exchanged a glance with Marianne. They were really getting somewhere now.

'What?' Angie said, noticing the look. 'What is it?'

It seemed that the previous day's events hadn't yet got around the whole of the institution.

'You haven't heard the news about Emily Roberts?'

'No, why, what's happened?'

Cullen delivered the line. 'I'm afraid she died, last night.'

Angie clamped a hand to her mouth.

'We have reason to believe that Ruben Wilkins might be able to help us with our enquiries,' he announced, trying to bring her back around.

'You think he...?'

'We think he might have been involved in her death,' was all he would say.

'I warned her,' she said. 'I told Emily what Ruben was like, that he was a cheater and a liar, what type of person he was. I warned her to get away from him.'

This was starting to make sense.

Angie looked like she was thinking hard about something. 'How did Emily...die?'

'She fell in front of a tube train last night,' he said.

This seemed to ignite something. 'He was following her,' she said, out of nowhere.

'What makes you say that?'

'I *should* have believed her,' she said, ignoring Cullen's question. 'Just the other day, Carly said she thought she'd seen him on the tube journey home. But she wasn't sure, and I said it must have been her imagination. You know, she's still been a bit all over the place, so I put it down to that.'

'Carly thought Ruben had been following her on the tube?' Cullen sought to clarify.

'Yes, well, she thought it might have been him. She said she thought she caught a glimpse of him, at Oxford Circus, but it was busy, and she just couldn't be certain. But it scared her.' She shook her head. 'I tried to calm her down, talked her out of those thoughts, you know, because I thought he was gone from her life. But if I'd believed her, then maybe this wouldn't have happened.'

'Please don't blame yourself,' Cullen soothed. 'We still don't know what happened last night.'

But the picture was definitely forming.

'Okay, okay,' she nodded, her inner turmoil still evident. 'I've got to warn Carly,' she said. 'In case he comes after her again.'

'We'll get someone around to Carly,' Cullen promised. 'To make sure she's okay.'

'Thank you, thank you.'

Then something that Angie had said came back to him. 'You said that someone else was asking about Ruben today?'

'Yes. A girl. Looking for Ruben Wilkins, where he lived.'

'Who was she?'

'Her name was Olivia. Olivia Byron. But I warned her too, to stay away from him. I told her what had happened with Carly.'

'Did you give her Ruben's address?'

She hesitated. 'I wasn't going to. But she was insistent. I think I've made another big mistake. I've put this girl in danger, haven't I?'

Cullen turned to Marianne. 'We need to act fast.'

She had the phone in her hand. 'I'm already on it.'

39

Cullen and Marianne hadn't even reached the tube station when DI Lomax called through with the big news.

'We've got him,' he announced.

'Really?' Cullen said, taken aback by the speed of the operation. It was barely fifteen minutes since they had put the call through. 'That was quick.'

Marianne stood near him, keen to know what was happening.

'A team was close by,' DI Lomax explained. 'They just called in. Wilkins was at home and they're with him now.'

'What about the girl? Olivia Byron?'

'Said that she came to see him, but she left the flat just before they arrived.'

'Do they believe him?'

'We're already checking CCTV along the road. And at the nearby tube station.'

'Notting Hill Gate?'

'Yes. We're pretty sure that's where she would be headed.'

'Good. So what did Ruben Wilkins say?'

'With regards to Emily Roberts, he's protesting his innocence – very vigorously, by all accounts.'

'We'll see what he has to say in the interview room,' Cullen noted, looking forward to facing this guy and getting to the truth.

The Professor had been wrong. Rarely did the truth simply emerge from the mist. You had to get in there, take that step into the unknown and find the truth, sometimes pull it kicking and screaming out of the depths.

He was good at that.

'There is other news,' DI Lomax said. 'I heard back from one of the control rooms, at Euston Square. Something that might be significant.'

'Go on...'

'An incident yesterday lunchtime, on the escalators. It would have come through to us, but they were still processing it. A man was up-skirting a female passenger, dropped his phone and was challenged by a member of the public. He got away, but the guys have a good image of the suspect.'

'Okay,' Cullen said, not knowing quite where this was going.

'In fact,' DI Lomax continued, 'they used the new facial recognition software and this guy pinged up several times over the past few weeks, relating to a number of ongoing stalking cases across the network. The best news is, they've already identified him after running the image through the national databases – his name is Henry Prince. He received a caution when he was seventeen, after being found in possession of a large amount of indecent images, although they were in the less severe category, relatively speaking.'

'Is this relevant to the case?'

'Henry Prince works in the same building as Ruben Wilkins, and the same small company as Olivia Byron.'

'Wow,' Cullen replied, trying to take in what this could all mean.

There had to be a connection, surely?

But what was it?

Cullen looked at DI McGuire, who was obviously desperate to be brought up to speed.

'Someone's been dispatched to pick up Henry Prince?' Cullen asked.

'They haven't as yet been able to locate him.'

'Okay, thanks for letting me know. Keep me updated. We're going to head back to Headquarters, so we'll see you soon if we don't hear from you before.'

'Sure, Boss.'

Cullen was just updating DI McGuire on the developments when he received another call. Assuming it was DI Lomax again, he whipped out the phone and answered without checking the caller ID.

'Danny, more news already?'

'It's Anthony,' Anthony Braddock said. 'I've got some *very* interesting news.'

There was obviously something in the air. 'Go on...'

'We decided to do some more work on your fallen angel case,' he said. 'Requested access to more of the street level cameras, tried to track your suspect as far as we could, see what we could find. We tracked them after the incident, for some miles. It took a while, but Transport for London were very helpful in providing the footage, and the effort was worth it.'

Cullen couldn't help but be excited.

This was where Ruben Wilkins would come unstuck.

'Don't keep me in suspense, Anthony. We don't want two heart attacks in one week.'

'Indeed we don't. Are you sitting down?'

'No, but let's just take the chance.'

'Okay. That mysterious person in the baseball cap. It's a woman.'

40

Olivia kept up her pace all the way back to the tube station, matching her heart rate, which was still running high. Throughout the entire fast walk she had chastised herself for confronting Ruben the way she did, and putting herself at risk.

Now she looked back on it, her actions had been reckless in the extreme. Stephanie had warned her against it, and she'd gone against the advice.

Nearly to her great cost.

Scanning through the barriers, and descending towards the platform, she allowed herself to relax a little as she waited for the next train, due in just three minutes.

But still, she couldn't help but reflect on the danger that she had put herself through.

And for what?

To try and get Ruben to change his ways?

There was obviously no chance of that.

Olivia glanced over at the stairs, for a moment wondering

if Ruben might have followed her. But why would he? She was now history to him. Thankfully.

But then a worrying thought hit her.

What if he stayed working in the café?

How would she deal with that?

That was another reason why she should have heeded Stephanie's warning, and just left things alone...

Two minutes until the train arrived...

She glanced over at the stairs again, as a middle-aged couple struggled down with two heavy-looking suitcases.

And behind them a young couple with backpacks.

She began to feel increasingly nervous again, as if the time left until the train arrived was linked somehow to a heightened chance of Ruben appearing.

One minute until the train arrived...

Olivia willed the train to come quicker. 'C'mon, c'mon.'

'Olivia!' someone said, right beside her.

Olivia recoiled, and very nearly screamed.

She'd never been so startled and actually felt physically sick with shock.

'Henry?' Henry Prince was standing next to her, appearing seemingly out of nowhere.

'Hi,' he replied, standing too close. 'Sorry, did I scare you?'

'Yes, yes, you did,' she said, trying to recover some composure.

'I'm really sorry. It wasn't my intention.'

'It's okay,' she said, feeling like it was anything but okay. 'What are you doing here?'

'Just exploring the area,' he said. He noted her disbelief. 'I do that sometimes – just explore London, you know, urban adventuring, people-watching, that sort of thing. I guess it's a hobby of mine.'

'But...aren't you supposed to be at the office?'

His face creased. 'Yes...yes I was supposed to be. But I took the afternoon off.'

The train rushed into the station, breaking the conversation.

Olivia noticed Henry take a step back as the train approached them, which was a little strange, as they were already well behind the yellow line.

Maybe he was nervous of the trains coming in at speed.

She looked at him, as a reassurance, and he smiled back anxiously. For a second she thought he was going to say something.

The train passed and slowed to a stop.

Olivia and Henry got on, standing at the corner, against one of the clear plastic partitions.

She was hugely relieved as the train set off, away from Ruben.

Blissfully unaware that someone *was* watching.

41

Cullen updated Marianne about the revelation from Anthony Braddock, that the person in the baseball cap had been a woman.

'They haven't identified her?'

'Not yet. Braddock's going to send through an image,' Cullen explained. He looked at his phone, impatient, willing the message to arrive.

How long could it take to send an email?

They headed towards BTP Headquarters, which was a comfortable twenty minute walk from their current location, just opposite Euston station.

But they only got as far as crossing the road when DI Lomax called with another update.

'Danny, you've got news for me?'

My God, he was standing at the scene of Tyrone Green's death!

Feeling uncharacteristically spooked by memories of the previous week, Cullen moved away to the grassy area in front of the station and turned his back to the road.

'Indeed I have,' DI Lomax said. 'The control rooms have

really pulled out the stops for us. They located Olivia Byron, entering Notting Hill Gate. She boarded an eastbound Central Line train. And she was with Henry Prince.'

'*What?*' Cullen said, shocked by the turn of events. 'We've got to intercept them.'

'Already on it, Boss,' DI Lomax said. 'Based on Olivia Byron's registered address, in Edgware, we're working on the assumption that she'll change at Oxford Circus, en route to Euston via the Victoria Line, and then the Northern Line through to Edgware.'

'Probably right,' Cullen said. 'So you've got officers ready at Oxford Circus?'

'There are a couple of uniforms on their way. They know what Olivia and Henry Prince look like.'

'Good.' Cullen was already moving towards the entrance to Euston station, and gestured for Marianne to follow him. 'We're at Euston now,' he said, 'in case they reach here.'

'Great! I'll forward you photos of them both now.'

They'd just entered the station concourse when Braddock's email arrived.

'Karen Roberts,' Cullen said, as he surveyed the image. He looked at Marianne. 'Emily's sister was the one following her?'

'Wow,' was all that DI McGuire could say.

But there was no time for discussion, and they headed down towards the underground.

42

'How is it going with your boyfriend?' Henry asked stiffly, as they continued the tube journey.

'My boyfriend? Ruben, you mean?' Olivia was surprised at Henry's line of questioning, as he'd never before spoken to her about such personal matters. But, as in previous encounters, she put it down to him just struggling to make conversation.

'Yes, Ruben.'

'He's not my boyfriend. We just went on a date, that's all.'

'Oh,' he replied, evidently surprised at the news. 'I thought you were...together.'

'No,' Olivia confirmed. 'We're not together.'

'But what about you being at his fla...' Henry began, before stopping himself. However, it was too late. He had given the game away.

'Were you following me?' Olivia asked, barely believing that this could be the case, but knowing it could be the only explanation for how Henry had known about her being at Ruben's flat.

'Yes,' he admitted, after some hesitation. 'I was following you. I'm sorry, Olivia. I know it might seem weird. But I can explain.'

'I'm not sure I want to hear it,' she said, longing to get away from everyone.

'Please, Olivia,' he pleaded. 'Just let me explain.'

'I really...'

'I have a confession to make,' Henry interrupted. 'I'm in love with you.'

Olivia shook her head. 'No, you're not, Henry.'

'I am!' he protested.

'How can you be?' Olivia challenged. 'We hardly know one another.'

'We've worked in the same office for years,' he said incredulously.

'Yes, but we don't really *know* each other, do we?'

He looked crestfallen. 'I thought we did.'

Another shake of Olivia's head. She couldn't quite believe what she was hearing, but yet as she looked at Henry's face, despite everything, she did feel pity for him.

She knew what it felt like, to be longing for love.

'I'm sorry, Henry.'

He seemed to think of something and his eyes brightened. 'The flowers,' he said, 'they were from me.'

'Oh, the flowers.'

They hadn't been from Ruben after all.

'And the message in the London Daily Post,' he added. 'The message was from me, to you. It was heartfelt. I really care for you, Olivia. I want to be with you. And I think we can make it work.'

'I'm sorry, Henry, you're a nice guy, but I just don't think about you like that.' Olivia didn't really want to say this, not here, but she felt that Henry had given her no other choice. 'I'm so sorry. Please, I hope you understand, and that we can still be friends?'

'Sure,' he said. But his storm-clouded face told her otherwise.

43

The train came to a stop and Henry and Olivia disembarked at Oxford Circus station. Henry was feeling sick to his stomach at the way their conversation had gone. It had been a disaster.

How could she have been so cruel?

So callous.

And all those lies about things being over with Ruben.

He had seen it for himself!

'See you tomorrow, Henry,' she said, although he barely heard the words. 'Look, Henry, I'm really sorry.'

Henry watched as Olivia walked away through the crowds to catch the train towards home. For a second he stood there, motionless, as the people flowed past him. He was inconsequential, insignificant, and ignored.

She was almost out of sight when he made his move.

This isn't over.

He glared up at the camera on the ceiling. It was pointing right at him, but that was good. It was just what he wanted.

There was no need to video on his phone this time.

Somebody else was doing the recording.

It wouldn't matter that the footage wouldn't be uploaded directly to the forum. His online friends would all see it anyway, on the mainstream news.

Maybe even those in America!

He stepped forward with newly found confidence and razor-sharp purpose.

It was time to revert back to his original plan.

44

Henry Prince was careful to keep his distance as he followed Olivia through the crowds to the Victoria Line's northbound platform. He enjoyed the feeling that she was completely unaware of his continued presence.

It made him feel powerful.

Olivia entered through the archway and turned right, along the platform.

Henry stalked after her, gazing up to where she was now standing.

To fulfil his fantasy he would have to get up close behind her, but he couldn't see how it would be possible without risk of her seeing him.

Damn it!

And then he noticed the other entrance, just behind where she was standing. He would need to go back out into the main walkway and re-enter via that alternative route. Then he would emerge in prime position, right behind her.

But the next train was due in under one minute.

He didn't have much time!

He hurried back out onto the walkway, but pulled up fast when he saw the two uniformed police officers striding purposefully in his direction.

He couldn't act now.

So he retreated back onto the platform.

Just as the train arrived.

45

Olivia was daydreaming as the train rushed into the station, thinking about the past few days.

How had things gone so wrong for her?

Just a day ago, everything had seemed to be on the up, and yet it had all come crashing down.

Ruben: the controlling, conniving individual who had sought to use her like he had used countless other women.

Henry: the strange work colleague who was now stalking her and declaring his undying love.

What a pair!

The train doors bumped open and she boarded, taking the free seat next to the exit.

What a life she had!

But as the train sped towards Euston, something unexpected happened.

She started to feel better.

Much better.

She had been treated badly. But she hadn't taken it lying

down. She had challenged them. She had stood up for herself.

Maybe now was time for a new start.

A new challenge.

She could look for another job, move out of London.

After all, there was no way she could continue sharing an office with Henry Prince.

Maybe she would head north.

Manchester. Liverpool. Newcastle.

She looked at her reflection in the opposite window and smiled.

She would come out of this stronger.

And as she stepped off the train at Euston she made a spur of the moment decision.

It was a lovely day and she had the urge to walk down by the Thames, rather than go back to her flat. After all, it was still quite early in the afternoon.

So she would head southbound instead.

46

'Still no sign,' Cullen said, as he and DI McGuire waited on the Northern Line's northbound platform. It was busy, as usual, so there was a chance that they had missed them, but Cullen felt confident that they would have spotted them.

DI Lomax had called through a few minutes ago with the disappointing news that they'd lost the pair at Oxford Circus.

Another train arrived, the third since they had been waiting here, and Cullen watched from the very edge of the platform, looking as far as he could along the length of the train to see if he could spot either Olivia or Henry boarding.

Nothing.

'They may not have taken this route,' Marianne said. 'I know this line is the most likely, but we don't know for sure that she's heading for home.'

Cullen nodded, thinking.

It was worth a try.

'You wait here,' he said, moving out into the walkway and jogging across to the southbound platform.

He entered at the far end, but immediately he saw a girl

who he recognised as Olivia Byron standing close to the edge, just behind the yellow line, half-way along the platform.

And behind her, Henry Prince.

A train was due any moment.

Cullen lengthened his considerable stride as he started to run.

47

Olivia waited on the southbound platform, her renewed optimism still burning brightly.

She was looking forward to taking a late afternoon walk down by the river, and thinking some more about her plans for the future.

Maybe she'd call Katherine, who lived down that way, and see if she was interested in grabbing a bite to eat at one of the riverside bars when she'd finished in the office.

The train emerged from the tunnel.

And that's when she saw something out of the corner of her eye.

Rushing towards her from behind.

Before she had chance to react, she was lifted off her feet by a high impact, and felt like she was flying through the air.

To her death. In front of a tube train.

She screamed as her body slammed into something solid.

There was a man on top of her!

'Detective Paul Cullen,' he said, moving his not insignificant weight off her. 'You okay?'

She managed to nod.

She could still hear screams, but they weren't hers.

'He just ran straight in front of the train!' she heard someone shout.

'Don't look,' the police officer warned her. 'Please, don't look.'

48

Cullen brought the two cups of tea into the living room at Philip's house and handed one to Sarah, who had her legs curled underneath her body on the sofa.

'I've been thinking,' Sarah said. 'If Tony hadn't had his heart attack, you wouldn't have been involved in the fallen angel investigation.'

'Must have been meant to be,' Cullen said, taking a sip from his drink.

'I guess.'

Cullen had returned up to Wigan early on Friday morning. He'd taken Thursday to sort out some loose ends regarding the case. Karen Roberts had been arrested and questioned about her role in her sister's death. She had admitted to having an affair with Ruben Wilkins, behind Emily's back. Karen had explained that several weeks before, Emily had suspected that someone was stalking her on the way to and from work, and was so spooked that she had decided to move back up to Scotland. This had suited Karen, who would then be able to be with Ruben without interference. However, when Emily changed her mind as the stalking fears subsided, and decided to stay in the capital, Karen had decided to frighten her in an attempt to ensure she did leave.

But the plan led to Emily's death, which Karen claimed she deeply regretted.

As for Ruben Wilkins himself, Danny and Marianne were dealing with him.

Meanwhile, there was the matter of Henry Prince's death. Without Cullen's rugby tackle intervention, it would have been Olivia who would have breathed her last breath that evening. As it was, she was holding up well, when he visited her the following morning. He had been pleasantly surprised by her resilience.

But Cullen still had unfinished business.

'Back there, at Acorn House,' he said, 'I realised what the real problem is. Sitting there with Philip, it all became clear.'

'Go on.'

He looked straight at his wife. 'I just didn't want to see Philip like that.'

'None of us do, Paul. It's upsetting for all of us.'

He shook his head. 'No, it's more than that. I realised, I didn't want to be with him, that person.'

Now her expression shifted slightly. 'I don't understand.'

Cullen searched for the right words. 'In my mind, I think I preferred to think that Philip was already dead. And the best way of maintaining that belief, was not to see him.'

Sarah's eyes were teary. 'But he's not dead, Paul. He might not remember events, he might not remember you, or me, but he is still alive. And he needs us.'

'I know,' he replied. 'I know that now. Looking into his eyes, I realised what an idiot I'd been.'

'You've not been an idiot, Paul. You've just been human.'

He nodded, knowing all about human frailties.

'The thing that Phil said,' Sarah continued, 'that came from deep within, from the Phil that we both know and love. He *really* meant it, Paul. You made a connection that even I haven't managed to make.'

'Do you really believe I can make a difference?'

She smiled. 'I've never been so certain of anything in my life.'

'So what now?' Sarah asked, as they walked arm and arm around the lake at the Three Sisters nature park, just ten minutes' drive from Philip's house. It was an area that had been reclaimed from the region's coal mining past, and had been transformed into a conservation site where rare butterflies and birds prospered.

Many times in the past, during Amy's toddler years, Cullen had brought his daughter to the play park, watching with delight as she squealed with excitement on the swings.

She'd loved the ducks and swans too.

It was a place of very happy memories. And a time when Amy was happy and carefree, long before those testing teenage times of anxiety and depression, when the weight of the world and her own thoughts had very nearly crushed the life out of her.

Cullen turned away from the play park, where a new generation of children were having the time of their lives, and brought himself back to the present.

Things weren't that bad now. Amy had got through the worst, surely.

But still, there would always be that doubt...

'I booked for the match tonight,' Cullen answered finally. 'For Phil and me. There's a meal after the game where you get to meet some of the players, past and present. It's run in association with the local dementia charity. I checked with Acorn House, and they're okay with him going.'

Cullen looked on expectantly, but was surprised by Sarah's muted reaction.

'You don't think it's a good idea?' he said, as they paused by the side of the lake.

Sarah went to speak but hesitated. 'It's...it's not that. It's just that, well, there's something I haven't told you...'

'Go on.'

'Yesterday, I took Philip out, just down the road to the supermarket, he'd been calm and I thought it would do him some good - he doesn't get much chance to get out. Things were going well until we got half way around and then he started trying to pull things off the shelves. When I tried to stop him, he got aggressive and...and he lashed out, more in frustration I think.'

'He hit you?'

'No. But if I hadn't moved quite quickly, I think he might have done.'

'Then what?'

'He got upset and we went straight back to Acorn House. We left the shopping in the trolley, in the store.'

'You should have told me.'

'I haven't told Acorn House. I daren't. I'm afraid they might kick Philip out if there are more incidents of aggression.'

Cullen nodded. 'I understand.'

Sarah was still thinking, torn at the potential positives

and negatives of Cullen's proposal. And then he could see her mind was made up.

'When we got back to Acorn House, I took him straight to his room. He was crying, Paul, but when I told him you were coming back to visit, he stopped and smiled. He actually smiled.'

Now it was her turn to tear up.

'Let's try it,' she said.

He took her by both shoulders and drew her near.

'It will be good,' he said. 'I just want to make things better.'

Sarah smiled. 'You know you can't solve every case, don't you?'

Cullen didn't reply.

49

Shazney Powell screwed her eyes tight shut as the coffin that contained her beloved Tyrone was carried into the church by his four friends.

She didn't dare open them, for fear that the sight of the wooden box would send her spinning to the ground.

'He can't be dead. He can't be dead. He can't be dead.'

She felt her father's arm around her back, and it did give her comfort. She let her head drop onto his shoulder, and she sobbed uncontrollably into his neck.

'Don't worry, Angel,' her father said. 'The man who did this to Tyrone. The man who did this to you. He's going to pay a very heavy price. A very heavy price indeed.'

<<<<>>>>

DETECTIVE PAUL CULLEN WILL RETURN...

ACKNOWLEDGMENTS

Thank you to everyone who has followed me in my author journey since 2011. Particular thanks to those on my mailing list and the members of my Facebook Group. Writing can be a solitary business, so it's great to have contact with such a generous and encouraging group of people!

I hope you enjoyed the second instalment of my Detective Paul Cullen mystery series. Paul Cullen will return in Dead Ahead.

Best wishes,

Paul

August 2020

ABOUT THE AUTHOR

Paul Pilkington is a British author of mystery, suspense and thriller novels. He is best known for his Emma Holden Suspense Mystery series, which follows the story of a young actress named Emma Holden who is thrown into a world of danger and intrigue after the sudden disappearance of her fiancé. Paul has also written several best-selling standalone novels, including For Your Own Protection and Someone to Save You, as well as the Detective Paul Cullen mystery series.

Paul's writing style is fast-paced, suspenseful, and character-driven. His novels explore complex themes and issues, such as love, loss, family, and redemption.

Visit Paul's website to find out more about his writing. You can also join his mailing list to receive the latest book news and updates:

www.paulpilkington.com

Printed in Great Britain
by Amazon

39002548R00158